Unwrapped

By Jaci Burton

He's going to give her the Christmas gift of her dreams...in triplicate.

When Justin Garrett accidentally views Amy Parker's private online journal, he sees the cold corporate exec in a brand new light. It seems the icy, unapproachable Amy has fantasies. Fantasies that both appall and intrigue her.

No one knows the real Amy Parker, and she's satisfied to keep it that way. A woman with kinky tastes wouldn't cut it in the straight-laced law firm where she's fought her way to partnership. And she certainly refuses to let an underling use her to advance in the firm. Justin Garrett might be brilliant, gorgeous, and sexy as hell, but he's firmly restricted to her fantasies and that's where he'll stay.

While working together on a corporate acquisition in Hawaii over the Christmas holidays, Justin sets out to make Amy's secret fantasy come true—a night of passion with two men who adore her. And he knows the ideal other man to help Amy unwrap the perfect Christmas gift.

But first he has to melt her heart and convince her he sees her as a woman, not a rung to climb on the career ladder. In fact, by giving Amy exactly what she's always wished for, Justin hopes to climb right into her heart.

This title contains the following: explicit sex, graphic language, ménage a trois, a trip to Hawaii and maybe a glimpse of Santa on a surfboard.

To Do List
By Lauren Dane

He wasn't part of her balance sheet. But one week in his bed could tip the scales.

Since she could pick up a pencil, Belle Taylor has used lists and charts to map out her life. When she achieves a goal, she marks it off her to do list. Simple. But now, just steps away from her corner-office, name-on-the-letterhead goal, she realizes that the life she thought she wanted may come at too high a price.

Exhausted, she retreats home for Christmas vacation to rethink her life, complete with all-new lists. What she hadn't expected is Rafe Bettencourt, her brother's best friend, the man who she thought only saw her as a pesky younger sister. But when he kisses her under the mistletoe, Belle finds herself with a whole new set of goals to balance with what she thought she always wanted.

Rafe knows Belle is trying to figure out what to do with her life. He also knows he's done loving her from afar, and he's not beneath making it as hard as possible for her to choose to return to San Francisco.

Because Rafe can make to-do lists too—and his plan is to seduce Belle back home where she belongs. At his side. And in his bed.

Warning, this title contains the following: Smokin' hot monkey love and naughty wish fulfillment, a few words you wouldn't say in your grandma's presence.

Holiday Seduction

A Samhain Publishing, Ltd. publication.

Samhain Publishing, Ltd.
577 Mulberry Street, Suite 1520
Macon, GA 31201
www.samhainpublishing.com

Holiday Seduction
Print ISBN: 978-1-59998-959-4
Unwrapped Copyright © 2008 by Jaci Burton
To Do List Copyright © 2008 by Lauren Dane

Editing by Angela James
Cover by Anne Cain

Unwrapped, ISBN 1-59998-841-0
First Samhain Publishing, Ltd. electronic publication: December 2007
To Do List, ISBN 1-59998-876-3
First Samhain Publishing, Ltd. electronic publication: December 2007
First Samhain Publishing, Ltd. print publication: November 2008

Contents

Unwrapped

Jaci Burton

Dedication

To Angie— As always, thank you for being open minded, patient and such a great editor. I love working with you.

And to Charlie, for all the obvious reasons. I love you.

Chapter One

The weekend before Christmas, and Amy Parker was going to spend it in Hawaii. How utterly romantic. Warm sands, miles of breathtaking ocean, fragrant flowers, the place of romance.

Though romance wouldn't be on her radar this weekend. She was going to be there for her job, not love. Work was her love, her romance.

How utterly dull—but necessary, if she was going to become senior partner at the firm. Work had to come first. It always had.

Amy stretched, stifling a yawn. She cast a quick glance over at Justin Garrett, her traveling companion and associate at the law firm. He'd been sound asleep and snoring for hours, his long legs stretched out, his head leaning against the side wall of the plane, arms crossed over his chest. Oh why not? It was just the two of them on the corporate jet. Not like he was bothering anyone. Except her. How the hell could he sleep when there was so much work to do?

She knew how. He'd let her do all the work while he dozed almost the entire five-hour flight from Los Angeles to Maui. After giving her no more than a half hour of his attention while they worked on contracts, he'd told her they could do the rest when they landed. He thought they were prepared and accused her of overthinking. Then again, he always did that to her.

Then he'd gone to sleep, while she'd spent the better part of two-and-a-half hours making sure all the legal documents were ready, that they hadn't missed any of the important items, and setting the agenda for their meeting with their client, Mitch Magruder. They'd worked months on the divestiture of one of Mitch's companies to a national sporting goods chain, and they needed to finalize this before year end. Mitch was on a tight schedule, which was why they were on a plane headed to Hawaii right before Christmas. She'd allow nothing to screw this up, including the man who slept next to her.

Slept next to her. When was the last time a man actually slept next to her? Too long to remember. Her sex ached with the need to be touched, to be filled with a hot cock. She blew out a sigh, aware she'd had to give up a lot in order to push her way into a partnership with the firm. Sex and relationships were big ones to sacrifice, but she'd done fine on her own. Besides, vibrators made no demands on her time. They were always ready and willing when she was and asked nothing in return.

She should have bought herself a new vibe for a Christmas gift.

She snorted, then took a quick glance over at Justin and shook her head, realizing that her laugh wouldn't have awakened him. That man could sleep anywhere. She'd worked enough projects with him over the past three years to know him inside and out. At twenty-eight, he was the firm's brightest young star. He'd hit the ground running and had already brought in a ton of new clients for McKenzie and Shoals Law Firm. David McKenzie, the managing partner at the firm, had told the rest of them they should model their work ethic after Justin.

So typical. She'd been working her ass off at the firm for eight years now. She was thirty-three years old, a junior partner, and all she heard about these days was Justin, Justin,

Justin.

Not that she was jealous. She was just as good...no, better than Justin Garrett. The firm was just stingy about awarding partnerships. Hell, it had taken her five years to make junior partner, her next goal in sight becoming a senior partner. And she knew damn well that McKenzie was looking to promote Justin to a junior partner this year.

Not that she cared. She didn't feel threatened in the least that he was their new golden boy. If things went well in this acquisition, she anticipated making senior partner by the end of the year. And nobody, especially Justin, would stop her.

She was Justin's superior. She'd caught his sideways glances at her, the sexual hunger lurking in his always aware, warm eyes. God knows she'd spent enough years getting hit on by young attorneys to know better than to let anyone's roaming eye catch hers. That's why she never, ever mixed business with pleasure.

Though if she was going to, Justin would be the one she'd do it with. There was something so inherently male and animalistic about him. He was like a predator, and she'd always enjoyed being prey. If they weren't connected by work she'd give serious consideration to having a hot sexual fling with him, even if he was five years younger than her.

In fact, if she didn't loathe his business tactics and smart-ass personality so much, she could easily fall in love with someone like him. Fiercely intelligent, Harvard law graduate, Justin was a go-getter with charm and an easy-going personality, and his looks would make any woman melt. Tall, lean muscled, he definitely worked out and it showed. Jet black hair and the sexiest whiskey eyes that revealed every one of his naughty thoughts.

Wouldn't he be shocked to know her thoughts? Everyone

saw her as the uptight ice queen of the firm. Cold, calculating and all about business.

If only things were different. If only she could let go, she might entertain a few of her wayward thoughts. But in business that spelled ruin, so she closely guarded her fantasies and real desires under her perfectly designed bitchy demeanor. It served her well.

But underneath she was seething with needs too long left unexplored. Her list of fantasies was long and detailed, but there was one she wanted more than anything. The likelihood of it happening was pretty damned slim given her current work and personal life.

Ha! What personal life? She hadn't even had an orgasm in three days. They'd been working nonstop on the acquisition and by the time she got home at night she fell into bed, too exhausted to even take a few minutes for a quick climax.

Glancing again at Justin, she wondered what he'd think if she pulled her panties off and masturbated right there next to him. The thought alone had her wet and throbbing. She shifted uncomfortably in the roomy seat, wishing she was by herself so she could get off. It wouldn't take long. Her nipples were already taut and tingling against her silk bra, the satiny fabric like a lover's caress against the aching buds. Heat pooled low in her belly, warming her sex with a low but very insistent flame.

The logical voice inside her head told her to slip into the bathroom and take care of her problem. The risky, wanton sex goddess inside her told her to pull a blanket over her lap, slip her panties off and make herself come right there in front of Justin.

No. God, no, she couldn't do that. What if he woke up and caught her? She'd be mortified, and probably fired once word got out that she was some kind of sick sexual deviant who not only masturbated in public but in front of a coworker.

Then again, she'd been typing like mad on the laptop, talking on the phone and mumbling to herself the entire time, and he hadn't budged an inch. He was probably one of those guys who entered a coma when he slept and nothing short of a bomb going off would wake him.

Fantasy and excitement won out over logic and caution. She reached for the blanket tucked into the side of her seat and covered the lower half of her body. Slipping off her heels, she kept one eye on Justin while she reached under her skirt. Her clit throbbed, tightening into a ball of aroused nerve endings when her fingers met the crotch of her panties.

Soaked. She was drenched with moisture already. She could probably strum her clit over her panties and come hard and fast. Yet that wicked part of her wanted her sex exposed, excited by the idea of being caught half-naked under the covers. Lifting her hips, she pulled her panties aside.

Keeping a wary eye on Justin, she picked up a book and opened it with one hand, so if he woke she could at least look like she was doing something. She used her other hand to draw her skirt up her thighs and spread her legs apart, cool air wafting over her heated pussy.

This was so wrong, so...naughty. It turned her on.

Inching her hand between her legs, she cupped her pussy, pressing the heel of her hand against her mound and sliding her fingers over her swollen slit and dipping them between her pussy lips. She bit down on her bottom lip to stifle the groan of pure ecstasy. Her sex was on fire, the need great as her clit throbbed and burned arousal deep in her womb.

Pressure built and skyrocketed fast as she kept her gaze trained on Justin. He hadn't moved at all. She took the opportunity to admire the fullness of his lips. Now that mouth could do amazing things to a woman's body. Her pussy spasmed at the vision of his lips covering her clit and sucking the bud until she screamed. Her gaze traveled down to his hands. Long, thick fingers she could already feel buried deep in her cunt. She drove her own fingers hard inside her pussy, feeling it grip them tight as if grasping for a lifeline against the wash of pleasure drowning her.

Unable to resist, she studied the crotch of his jeans, spying the telltale bulge pressing against the denim. She grinned. He had a hard-on. She wondered what he was dreaming about?

What if he woke right now? Would he brush her hand out of the way and lean over the seat to press his mouth against her aching sex? She lifted her hips just thinking about offering her pussy to his delectable lips so he could feast on her until she came against his mouth.

She was close. So very close. Biting back the whimpers threatening to escape her throat, she focused on the touch of her fingers, withdrawing them to paint creamy juices over her clit, strumming it rapidly with her palm, drawing ever closer to that moment. Soon, so soon, almost there...

...now! Oh, yes, she was coming! The silent scream tore through her mind as she fought to keep from thrashing around the chair in the throes of a blindsiding orgasm. She let the book fall into her chair and gripped the arm of the seat tight, riding out the waves of her climax until she felt so lightheaded she remembered to breathe again.

The sound of her panting breaths was the only thing she heard beyond the quiet droning of the engines. Shuddering, she forced great gulps of oxygen into her lungs, desperately wishing she could strip naked and straddle Justin's hard cock.

But that wasn't to be. That wasn't the person she wanted him to see. Instead, she smoothed her skirt down and headed for the bathroom to clean up, thankful that at least she'd gotten through it without Justin waking up.

Wouldn't that have been an eye opener for him. What would he have thought if he'd caught her?

She shuddered at the thought. He'd probably think she was a depraved pervert, and then he'd tell everyone at the firm.

As she shut and locked the bathroom door, she stared at her expression in the mirror. Her face was flushed, her bottom lip reddened from the force of biting down on it.

You've got to be more careful in the future, Amy. These fantasies of yours are going to be your downfall some day.

Much better if Justin continued to think of her as cold and unapproachable. She'd make sure he never discovered that underneath her staid, icy exterior burned the heart and libido of a wild woman. A wild woman with some pretty bold fantasies.

Justin finally exhaled when Amy closed the door to the restroom.

Holy shit! His cock was so hard he could beat it with a hammer and it wouldn't faze him. His balls were drawn tight against his body and ached for release. He was ready to explode.

Amy had surprised him. No, that wasn't even close. She'd shocked the hell out of him.

When he'd inadvertently viewed her email on her business laptop the other night, he laughed it off, thinking it couldn't be true. No way could staid, buttoned-up Amy Parker have a hot fantasy like that. He'd dismissed it as some bullshit conversation she'd had with her best friend.

But the idea had stayed with him and refused to go away. By the time they boarded the plane, he'd had a tentative plan worked out in his mind. After what he'd just witnessed, he was more convinced than ever that she was hiding some wicked, nasty little desires.

And he intended to be the man to make those desires a reality.

He winced and adjusted his crotch. The scent of her arousal still filled the air. It would take a long time to forget the sounds of her movements, the wet sucking noises her fingers fucking her pussy had made and the visuals those sounds had created in his mind.

It was all he could do not to slide his hand under her blanket and take over for her. He wished his tongue had been buried deep in her mouth, eyes wide open, watching her face as she went over the edge.

So far, this trip was going much better than he'd hoped. The other night when they were putting the final touches on the acquisition papers, she'd grumbled about him doing his part and pointed to her laptop, then left to grab a bite to eat.

So he'd sat at her desk and clicked on what he'd thought was the legal file. When he went looking for an attachment to go with it, he clicked on her email, figuring it was there. Instead, he wound up picking his tongue off the floor when what popped up was an email she'd been writing to her friend, Gloria. It was an accident, one he knew she'd kill him for if she discovered he'd read it. He really meant to close it as soon as he realized the mistake, but that first line...hell, who could have or would have stopped after reading that?

He still remembered every word of it. Not the short reply from her girlfriend, Gloria, but the original email Amy had sent her that had trailed the bottom of Gloria's reply:

Give me a break, Gloria! Just who the hell am I going to have a ménage with? Vibrator A and Vibrator B?

I wish. I just don't have time to meet men. And the ones I do meet I work with. I certainly can't fuck one guy I work with, let alone two.

That's the bad thing about making your job your life. I have no dates, no relationships, and the only guy I want to fuck is five years younger than me and I work with him! Besides, he's an arrogant prick. He just so happens to be an arrogant prick with a devilish smile, hot whiskey eyes and a body I want to lick from top to bottom.

Sigh I really need to get laid. Hell, at this point one guy would be good enough.

I'll work on having two at a time someday. When I'm eighty or so. *snicker*

Let's have drinks tomorrow night before I leave for Hawaii. How about eight at McConnell's Pub?

Love you!

Amy

He'd known right away she was talking about him. They'd been sparring ever since he started working for the firm. She resented the fact he'd climbed the corporate ladder faster than her, but he never understood her animosity or feeling of competitiveness with him. She was damned brilliant. Law degree from Stanford, top of her game in the legal field. In spite of her tough-bitch attitude, she'd taught him a lot. Now was his chance to be the teacher.

From the first time he'd seen her strolling down the hall, he'd wanted her. Her auburn hair had been pinned tightly in a respectable upsweep, her conservative black suit falling all the way to her knees. She exuded the persona of cold, impersonal lawyer.

But her eyes gave her away. They oozed passion and desire. The way she looked at him sometimes, like she was so hot to fuck him, made him wonder what was on her mind. Sometimes it took sheer mind over matter to keep his dick from tenting against his suit coat.

Like the episode in the plane just now. He wondered who she'd been thinking about when she masturbated. Since she mentioned him in her note to her friend, had she been thinking about him? Was she thinking about her fantasy ménage? And if so, who were the two guys?

He jammed his fingers through his hair and stared out the window. Too much thinking made him crazy. Hell, *she* made him crazy! And she'd been doing it for years, acting like she couldn't stand the sight of him while at the same time shooting him surreptitious glances that revealed a desperate sexual hunger.

Despite her possible desire for him, he'd kept his distance. Since he wasn't certain she really wanted him, he didn't want to risk a potential sexual harassment suit as a way for her to get rid of him. Besides, he didn't want to slide her panties off and fuck her until she screamed because she was a way to advancement at the firm.

He didn't need her help for that. No, he wanted Amy for an entirely different reason altogether.

She was smart, beautiful and obviously dying for some really hot sex. And because she kept herself as busy as she did, he knew the really hot sex department was suffering.

But he had a fix. He'd just have to convince her that he could give her what she needed and that he had no ulterior motives in doing so.

He looked up at the sound of the bathroom door. Their

gazes met and she paused, her eyes widening for a fraction of a second before her cool, professional face settled back into place. She slipped into her seat and glared at him.

"Nice nap?" she asked, disdain in her tone.

"Yeah. Had some wicked hot dreams, too."

He caught the telltale blush on her cheeks as she shot him an icy glare. "Spare me the gory details and take a look at these documents I worked on while you were having your long nap."

She pushed the laptop toward him and shuffled through her briefcase, effectively ignoring him.

He grinned, opened the document and scanned it quickly. Of course everything was in order. Amy never made mistakes. She'd long ago perfected a competent, don't-fuck-with-me attitude.

That was about to change, because he was definitely going to start fucking with her.

The Magruder Sports Company wasn't the only thing that was about to be acquired in Hawaii.

Justin had an acquisition of an entirely different sort in mind.

Chapter Two

Amy waited outside her bungalow for Justin. Since his room was next door, he'd told her they could meet before heading to the main hotel for dinner with Mitch.

They'd been assigned adjoining bungalows instead of rooms in the main hotel. The bungalows were spacious and right near the edge of the beach. The setting sun shimmered over the water, casting it a glittering gold. A handful of swimmers still hung out on the beach to catch the last rays of sun.

What a great place to spend the Christmas holidays. If only she was on vacation.

Instead of enjoying the water, she'd spent the afternoon at the resort gift shop, buying new clothes. She took a quick glance at her red and yellow flowery sundress, feeling a bit too casual for a business dinner. But Mitch had insisted they wear casual clothes instead of business suits. And he was right. It was entirely too warm for anything else but minimal clothing and she hadn't had time to shop before they'd left Los Angeles.

"Well, that's a new look for you."

She turned at the sound of Justin's voice, as always, a small hitch interrupting her normal breathing pattern whenever she looked at him. Typically he wore business suits, but today was different. Much different. The white tank top and royal blue shorts showed off his tanned, well-muscled arms and legs. Way more than she'd ever seen of him, making her wonder how it would feel to slide her hands under his shirt and palm his chest. Shaking off thoughts of moving her hands even lower on his sculpted body, she asked, "You're really wearing *that* to a business dinner?"

He grinned, showing off straight, white teeth that seemed even whiter against his dark skin. He must have been out in the sun today. "I've known Mitch for a lot of years. Trust me, he'll be wearing the same thing. And you," he added, tilting his head and perusing her skimpy sundress, "look damn hot in that dress. Quite a departure from your typical buttoned-up look."

Ignoring his comment as well as the internal heat shooting through her nerve endings, she said, "Shall we go?"

He nodded and stepped beside her as they made their way along the walkway leading to the main hotel. The Royal Surfer Hotel was a sprawling resort with twin white towers curved toward each other. They passed three swimming pools on their way into the main entrance, all filled with laughing children and very relaxed looking adults.

Along with his sporting good interests, Mitch owned this hotel as well as a few others on neighboring islands. His decision to concentrate on the hotel business was the reason they were meeting to finalize the divestiture of Magruder Sports.

The scent of gardenias filled the air around her and she inhaled, enjoying the smell of fresh, clean air. You didn't dare take too deep a breath in Los Angeles, otherwise you might choke on the smog.

This, on the other hand, was paradise. She might not be on vacation, but she still intended to enjoy every moment of her visit to Maui.

The lobby of the hotel was pristine, decorated in white marble and pale, whitewashed wood interspersed with flowering tropical plants and waterfalls.

Mitch was waiting for them by the dolphin waterfall. As always, Amy felt a pure rush of feminine appreciation when she saw him. At forty-two, he had the body of a man fifteen years younger, no doubt due to the time he spent surfing. The only evidence of his age was a slight graying at the temples. Otherwise, his hair was still a rich, midnight black, his face darkly tanned from years in the sun, and his eyes such a vivid, turquoise blue any woman looking at him would do a double take.

"Hey, gorgeous," he said, kissing her on the cheek. "Glad you took my clothing suggestions seriously."

She smiled. "I always do what a client asks."

Mitch arched a brow, his gaze flitting quickly to Justin, who grinned and shook Mitch's hand. "Hey, buddy. Long time. Sorry I missed the last meeting, but I was finalizing another case."

Mitch shook his head and motioned them toward a long breezeway. "You're always too busy, Justin. You should still be working for me here in the tropics instead of that overpopulated plastic Los Angeles."

Justin laughed. "You didn't need my help back then. Besides, you already had an army of attorneys. How the hell was I supposed to shine in that crowd of sharks?"

"Still out to be number one, huh?"

"You know me."

"Yeah, I do. And it suits you. Though I still think you should come work for me again."

As always, Amy felt like an unwanted third whenever she and Justin met with Mitch. Justin had apprenticed for the legal department of one of Mitch's corporations while in college before coming to work for McKenzie and Shoals. They were close, almost like brothers, even though they weren't close in age. But their easy, relaxed camaraderie was always a bit disconcerting. She wasn't used to sitting back and being quiet. That wasn't her style at all.

The Tiki Lounge stood high on a deck overlooking the ocean. The swirling breeze provided a cooling respite from the humidity as they walked outside and were seated at a table cornering the outdoor restaurant.

"Mai Tais," Mitch announced to the waitress, holding up three fingers before turning his attention on Amy. "Hope you don't mind eating here. I hate being stuck inside the offices or the suite. Nothing like fresh air and a Hawaiian sunset to relax after a hard day. Besides, if I know you, you haven't been outside much yet."

"I spent the afternoon at the gift shop."

"There's a surprise," Justin said. "I thought you'd spend it working."

If she hadn't needed clothes, she would have. "I'll work later tonight."

Their drinks arrived and when Amy took a sip, she grinned at the tangy, fruity flavor. "Oh, this is good." She'd always been a sucker for a sweet drink. It was like having a forbidden dessert.

Their business was discussed over drinks, all the last-minute details ironed out. They had only to go over the documents tomorrow to finalize everything and make arrangements for the transfer of assets to complete the deal.

Amy spied a couple strolling along the water's edge, the woman wearing a simple white shift, a row of flowers in her hair. She held a bouquet. The man had on a white linen suit.

"Newlyweds," Mitch said with a grin. "Lots of people come

here to get married. You'll see a ton of them."

Amy nodded. "Uh-huh." She really should have bought a new vibrator.

"Hawaii is all about sex and romance, you know," Mitch said. "Must be something in the air."

Amy shifted and squeezed her legs together, determined to quell the throbbing of her clit. She would *not* think about sex. "So, Mitch, are you satisfied with the arrangements for the acquisition?"

Mitch laid his hand over hers. "Amy, relax. The acquisition is fine. There's nothing left to do but paperwork." He gave her fingers a light squeeze. "You really need to let loose and enjoy yourself, breathe in the Hawaiian air, have another Mai Tai."

Let loose? "Mitch, I appreciate the sentiment, really. But Justin and I are here to work. For you. We're not on vacation."

"There's not much paperwork left to do except going over the finer details and making sure everything's signed," Justin said. "Mitch is right, Amy. Have fun while you're here and relax."

Easy for him to say. He took everything lightly, as if he didn't have a care in the world. Amy was serious about her job, her career, advancing up the corporate ladder. This acquisition had to go down perfectly.

"Don't you ever unwind?"

"Of course I do."

Mitch leaned back in his chair. "Really. And what do you do for fun?"

"I work out at the gym."

Justin snorted. Amy shot him a glare.

"That's relaxing to you?" Mitch asked.

"It releases the tension and keeps me in shape."

"Well, there's no doubt you're in shape, but there are much better ways to release tension."

Oh, God. She didn't even want to think of all the "better" ways she could release tension, and she wasn't about to discuss the other ways she released, especially in the privacy of her bedroom. And she especially didn't want to start thinking about said release while in the company of two very sexy men. Her fantasies were vivid enough without sending her mind into overdrive.

She took a long swallow of her drink. It was sweet, so she took another, quenching her thirst until the glass was empty. At least one of her thirsts, anyway. Mitch signaled the waitress and in short order she had another full drink. Yummy.

"Damn, Mitch, I should have never left your side," Justin said, tipping his glass toward him. "You've made one hell of a life for yourself."

"Thanks. So much a life that I have to unload some of the business side of it so I have a chance to enjoy a few of the fruits of all the years of labor."

"That's why you have us," Amy said. "To help you divest some of your hard work. It's time for *you* to relax a little and unburden yourself."

Mitch laughed. "I'm hardly ready to head out to pasture yet, Amy."

Amy sat straight in her chair, realizing her blunder. "Oh. Of course not. That's not what I meant at all. I mean, for someone your age you're in phenomenal shape. Most guys half your age don't look as good as you."

She realized she was babbling, and in a really inappropriate way. Why didn't she just crawl into his lap, lick him all over and just complete the humiliation?

Her cheeks flushed hot, her eyes widened, and Mitch

27

grinned.

Jesus, could he read her mind?

"I'm sorry," she said. "Long flight, not much sleep and...what's in these drinks anyway?" She pushed the offending cocktail to the center of the table.

Mitch pushed it back in front of her. "Amy, chill. I'm the last person to be insulted. I want you and Justin to have a good time here. I'm a pretty laid back kind of guy. You can say, or do, anything you want."

He wasn't helping by saying things like that.

"Now that's a tempting offer," Justin said, slanting his gaze to Amy. "And Mitch is right, Amy. You do need to unwind."

Amy's gaze shifted back and forth between Justin and Mitch, and her fruity-drink-addled brain went foggy.

Oh, yeah. That could be fun and a fantasy come true. Sexy, forbidden Justin, the man who'd fueled her fantasies for years, and rugged, outdoorsy Mitch, older, experienced...

"It's hot out here," she mumbled. "And I should get some food into my empty stomach to counteract the effects of these cocktails."

"Oh I don't know," Justin said. "I kind of like you loosened up and under the effects of alcohol."

The warmth of Justin's gaze was unnerving. She fought it by using her normal antagonistic attitude, her only armor against him. "You would. Wouldn't it advance your agenda?"

Normally Justin would tell her that his interests were purely professional. This time, he leaned across the table. She took a deep breath and inhaled the fresh, just-showered scent of him.

"Actually, I do have an agenda where you're concerned, Amy. But it has nothing to do with business."

Before she could react to that bold statement, Mitch laid his hand on her forearm, and she dragged her shocked gaze away from Justin.

"It's not hot out here, Amy," Mitch said. "There's a cool breeze coming off the water. I think it's just you."

Amy stared straight into Mitch's piercing blue eyes, and melted.

Between the two of them, she was going insane. Cool breeze, hell. She'd like to crawl onto cool sheets, naked. With both of them.

She was in so much trouble. And it had nothing to do with the cocktails.

Chapter Three

Justin fought back a grin. Amy was definitely wavering, and he didn't think it was entirely due to the alcohol.

Damn, she looked beautiful with her hair down, the breeze blowing the strands away from her face. Moonlight glowed on her bare shoulders, and he wanted to press his lips to them, work his mouth from there to her neck, then everywhere else. He'd bet she'd taste like strawberries. Every time she walked by him she smelled like strawberries.

She may act like the no-nonsense, straight-laced corporate professional, but she smelled damn edible and she was driving him crazy, because she had everything he wanted in a woman— intelligence, independence, beauty and she knew exactly what she wanted out of life.

There was nothing he'd change about her.

Okay, maybe one thing. He wanted to be included in those things she wanted in her life. She worked too damn hard and she never played, never had a serious relationship, always got involved with the wrong kind of guys.

Correction—she never got involved at all. She used men as arm candy, but she never had relationships. Her life was her work and Justin meant to change that, because he'd been guilty of the same thing.

Because too much work and not enough play wasn't getting either of them what they wanted. He wanted Amy, she wanted him, and she also wanted a ménage.

And Justin intended to give Amy a very special Christmas present this year. But first, he was going to have to figure out just how far he could go with Amy, because his intent wasn't to push her into something she really didn't want or wasn't ready for.

Though he had a pretty good idea it wouldn't take much pushing.

In fact, he intended to start tonight. But first, it was going to be just the two of them. He was greedy—he wanted Amy all to himself.

They ate dinner, discussed a little business, and had more drinks. Amy seemed to relax, which was a good thing. He'd been hoping this trip to Hawaii would help her loosen up a little, and even for the first day, it was working. By the time the four-day trip was over, he planned to have her completely stress-free.

"So we'll meet in your office in the morning to sign all the paperwork?" Amy asked Mitch.

Mitch nodded. "I'll surf in the morning, so how about ten?"

"Ten works," Justin said. "It'll give me time to take a run on the beach and clean up before we head to your office."

"Great." Mitch pushed back from his chair, lifted Amy's hand and pressed a kiss to it. "Have a little fun and don't work so hard. I'll see you in the morning."

Justin noted Amy's gaze was riveted on Mitch as he kissed her hand. The heat in her eyes didn't escape him. The odd thing was, he felt no jealousy, because when she looked at Mitch it was lust. When she looked at him, yeah there was definitely lust in her eyes, but something more than that. He couldn't really explain it, it was just...different. He supposed he'd have to explore that. With her. Starting tonight.

After Mitch left, Amy pushed her chair back. "I think I'll call it a night." He noticed she was weaving just a bit.

"I'll go with you. You look a little unsteady on your feet."

She managed a little smile. "Those fruity cocktails pack one hell of a wallop."

They hadn't made it more than a few steps outside the restaurant when Justin realized Amy was more than a little bit hammered. Not enough to have her stripping and jumping into the ocean naked, sadly, but enough that her typical inhibitions were long gone.

Good. Not that he'd take advantage of her in her inebriated state.

Much.

She weaved and crashed into him.

"Shit," she mumbled, blowing her hair out of her eyes. "Sorry."

He lifted her so he carried more of her weight. "Darlin, you're toasted."

She stopped, tilted her head back to stare at him. "I am not. I just didn't eat enough today."

"Which means the alcohol got to you."

She waggled her brows. "Maybe a little. It feels good. I need to do this more often."

A-freakin-men to that. He liked the feel of her body pressed up against him. Normally she kept her distance. More than kept her distance. Like the other side of the room if possible. Now she was close. Close enough for him to smell her skin, feel the softness of her body as he held her waist and maneuvered her along the walkway toward their rooms. He'd been waiting a long time for this.

When he got to her door, he held out his hand. "Key."

She fished into the tiny bag and drew it out. He opened her door and walked her inside, kicking the door shut behind him.

"Where are the damn lights?" she mumbled.

"Here." Justin flipped the switch and the room was bathed in the soft glow of the light from the lamp on the nearby table.

She tossed her purse on the table and turned to him. "Thanks. Not sure I could have found my room without your help."

"You're welcome." He marched into the tiny kitchen and pulled open the refrigerator.

"What are you doing in there?"

He came back with a bottled water and unscrewed the top. "Diluting you."

She snorted. "Oh. Good idea." She took the bottle and drank down half the water in it, then wiped her wet lips with her fingers. "The sweet drinks also make me thirsty. I don't know what I was thinking."

"Don't worry about it. It's not like you danced on the tables naked."

"God forbid."

She walked to the back door and slid it open, then stepped out onto the patio. Justin followed.

Amy blew out a breath and fell into one of the cushioned chairs.

"Better?"

"Yes. The air and the water helped. Thanks."

If he was a gentleman, he'd leave her alone. He didn't want to leave her alone and he sure as hell wasn't a gentleman. He slipped into the other chair.

The night was quiet and there was a breeze that blew strands of her hair. Moonlight shined down on her and she looked like a goddess sitting there just waiting for a man to worship her.

She deserved a little worship.

"I never relax like this," she said, staring out into the darkened sea.

"I know."

She turned to him. "I'm too anal. I can't separate my work life from my private life. My work has become my entire life. That shouldn't be. I should have a life, shouldn't I?"

"Yes."

She leaned back and planted her hands on the wide arms of the chair. "This is nice. The water, the sweet smell of the flowers, the music from the club across the way. I might sit here all night."

He stood. "Dance with me."

"What?"

"You said you wanted to relax, to start enjoying life a little. Start now. Dance with me."

She opened her mouth. Justin knew she was going to object, had a litany of excuses why she couldn't...or wouldn't. He held out his hand. "Dance with me, Amy. Let yourself go."

Let yourself go. Those three words were foreign to Amy. She'd never done that, especially in public, with a man. Everything was scripted. She'd always been in control, knew exactly what she was doing.

So when had she lost control tonight? Probably after her first drink. Now Justin was in her room, and there was moonlight and ocean breezes and she felt just a little bit too relaxed to be doing this.

Yet why not? The music was soft, they were in Hawaii and it wasn't like he'd asked her to have sex. What was the harm in dancing? She took the hand he offered and he drew her against his chest. His other arm came around her back and she resisted the urge to sigh out loud. It felt good. His body was rock solid, he was a lot taller than her and she had to tilt her head back to look at his face.

Whoa. Those eyes. It was one thing to stare into those warm whiskey eyes from across the board room, another thing to be so damn close she could drown in them.

"You okay?" he asked, moving with ease across the spacious patio.

"Yes." No. She wasn't okay. She had goose bumps. Her nipples were hard. Her panties were damp and she felt all too...desirable—female—hot. And she was in the arms of the wrong man, the man who fueled her fantasies, the one man she shouldn't be with. Career disaster.

"Justin..."

"Quit thinking, Amy," he said, palming her lower back and smiling in a way that Amy found devastating. "Nothing's going to happen that you don't want, so stop worrying. We're just dancing."

Maybe *he* was just dancing. She was self-combusting. His hands roamed her back, burning her with every touch. She might as well be naked. God, she really wanted to be naked, to feel flesh on flesh.

"Tell me what you're thinking," he whispered, his lips brushing her ear.

Her eyes drifted shut and she imagined him pulling down the straps of her dress and pressing his lips against her flesh. Scorching, searing her from the inside out. She wanted it so badly she could almost feel it. His breath was hot against her neck. She was trembling. She couldn't tell him what she was thinking.

"I'm thinking it's late and we have a meeting in the morning."

He stilled, pulled away, his smiling expression telling her he didn't believe for a second that's what she'd been thinking about. His mouth was so close she could breathe him in. One inch closer and she could feel his lips pressed against hers, could live the fantasies she'd only dreamed about for so long.

Instead, he stepped back and the spell was broken. "You're right. Get some sleep and I'll pick you up on the way to breakfast in the morning."

He turned and walked away, letting himself out. Amy couldn't make her feet move. Disappointment washed over her. He'd left her. Just like that. No argument, no attempt to seduce her. God knows it wouldn't have taken much effort. She was practically liquid. She'd have been easy.

Too easy.

Now she was a quivering mess of turned-on woman with no outlet to relieve this anxiety. And no way was she going to do it herself. Not when one extremely hot man occupied the bungalow next to hers.

With a shuddering sigh, she stepped inside, determined to obliterate thoughts of Justin from her mind.

She heard the sounds of Justin moving about in his room, her mind conjuring up visuals of him stripping out of his clothes, climbing into his bed, his cock hard as he took it in his hand and jacked off thinking about what he might have done with her.

Oh, God, Amy, where is your common sense? Hadn't she been spending years steeling herself against the possibility of this happening? Then one trip to Hawaii and a couple fruity cocktails and all her good intentions had gone down the drain?

Sleep. She needed rest and a clear head. By tomorrow, this would all be forgotten and she'd be herself again.

If she could sleep tonight. She got ready for bed, slid between the sheets and stared out her door, listening to the undulating waves crashing against the shore, wishing it were Justin crashing against her body.

Yeah, right. There'd be no sleep for her tonight.

Why the hell hadn't he taken what she would have so obviously given him?

What the hell was wrong with him anyway?

Justin's dick had been rock hard all night. Really not conducive to getting a good night's sleep. He at least hoped Amy had suffered a bit, too. When he left her, she'd been damn near panting, her cheeks flushed, her nipples like tight pebbles against her flimsy little sundress. Her lips had been parted in silent invitation. If he'd moved in and pressed his mouth to hers, she wouldn't have objected.

It had taken all his willpower to walk away from her. But he wanted her to know that he didn't just consider her a fuck. He wanted her sober and clear headed when he took her to bed. Amy had to make the decision, to know exactly what she was doing.

He hoped it wouldn't take long. In fact, he intended to give her the full court press today. He knocked at her door at nine-thirty a.m. She opened the door, a little tinge to her cheeks as she greeted him.

"Morning," she said.

"How's it going?"

She grimaced. "I have a headache. No more fruity cocktails

for me."

He laughed. "Sorry. Should have warned you about those. Stick to straight alcohol from now on."

"I'll keep that in mind. I just need to grab my jacket. Come on in."

He stepped in, leaning against the door and watching as she filled her briefcase. She wore a short skirt today, along with a well-fitting sleeveless silk blouse that she quickly covered up with a jacket. Buttoned it. All three buttons, too.

"Amy, it's too warm for that outfit."

"We're going to Mitch's office today. I'm dressing appropriately."

He rolled his eyes. "You know Mitch is informal."

"But I'm not." She grabbed her briefcase and joined him at the door. "Ready?"

He lifted his laptop case. "I have everything here. We've been ready for this for months. Just relax. It'll be over soon and then we can kick back and enjoy ourselves."

She gave him a wary look. "Uh-huh. I'll relax when the papers are signed and the merger is complete. That's what we're here for."

That's what she thought.

Magruder, Inc.'s office was located on the twenty-seventh floor of the main hotel. It was a short walk down the cement path and through the main lobby to the elevators. Amy was quiet throughout the walk. Justin wondered if her mind was on business or something else. It had to be something else. Typically before a client meeting she'd chatter nonstop, making sure they had everything lined up, that nothing would go wrong. It was completely uncharacteristic of her to go dead quiet like this.

A smiling receptionist wearing the clothing of aloha greeted them and showed them to the conference room. Justin opened his laptop while Amy busied herself with spreading out the paperwork Mitch would have to sign.

Mitch stepped in, dressed about the same as Justin in casual slacks and a polo shirt. Justin grinned and shook his hand.

"Mornin," Justin said.

"Hey," Mitch said, then turned to Amy. "Did you two have fun last night?"

Amy straightened, her gaze shooting to Justin. "Fun? What do you mean?"

"I mean did you enjoy the sights, take in one of the clubs, go for a night cruise? Anything?"

"Oh. No. We left right after you did."

Mitch shook his head. "Amy. I refuse to let you leave this island until you unwind a little."

She smiled. "I am unwound, Mitch. Honest."

"Uh-huh. We'll see about that. Justin and I might have to do this together."

Amy's eyes widened. "Do what together?"

"Relax you, of course."

"Shall we get started?" she asked, though there was a definite waver in her voice.

"Sure." Mitch sat at the head of the table and Amy and Justin took him step by step through the paperwork. A tedious, but necessary process of going through each page.

"Is it warm in here?" Amy asked, unbuttoning her jacket.

"Yeah," Mitch said, pushing back from his chair and moving toward Amy. "There's a glitch in the air conditioning system. I've got people coming over today to fix it. You should lose your jacket."

Justin didn't bother hiding his smile. This should be good.

Chapter Four

Amy supposed that fighting Mitch for her jacket wouldn't be a good idea. She would look ridiculous. She allowed him to slip it off her shoulders and drape it over the back of her chair. Damn it, why hadn't she worn a thicker bra today, or a less revealing blouse? Or fewer clothes? And why was Justin smiling at her like that?

And where the hell was her normal concentration?

And why was it so goddamn hot in here? And what the hell was wrong with her nipples? It wasn't cold, so why were they standing up like beacons?

Jesus. Her brain was mush. She had to get control. Her mind had been wandering all through the signing. She hadn't been able to focus at all, except on the two men flanking her. And her thoughts had not been centered on business. It was a damn good thing she could walk through an acquisition in her sleep, that she knew the paperwork backwards and forwards. Otherwise, she'd be so screwed right now. So far she'd been able to cover adequately. But when Mitch had pulled her jacket off, his fingers brushing her bare shoulders, and Justin gave her that knowing smile as if he knew exactly where her thoughts had been...

Surely she was imagining it all.

Forcing her mind back into work, they continued walking Mitch through the paperwork, though it was Justin who carried the meeting. Despite her intent, Amy couldn't concentrate. Well, that wasn't entirely accurate. She was concentrating. On Justin's mouth. And Mitch's strong, large hands. The easy camaraderie the two men shared.

Would the two of them mind sharing anything else? Like maybe her?

Dear God, Amy, get a grip.

And it was still hot in here!

It didn't help that Justin kept sliding glances her way, his gaze heated. And then Mitch would look at her, gracing her with a knockout smile that made her toes curl. And they both noticed her breasts straining against her blouse, the way her nipples stood at attention. She might as well strip naked and lay spread-eagled on the conference table so they could take turns fucking her.

Thoughts like that were not helping.

"Are you all right?" Mitch asked.

"Excuse me?"

"You groaned, Amy," Justin said.

Oh, shit. "I did?"

"Yes." Mitch stood. "I know it's warm in here. Let's take a swim."

Amy's eyes widened. "A swim? Mitch, we're not finished here."

"So? We'll finish later. The heat in here is brutal. We need to cool down. It's almost lunchtime anyway. We'll meet at the beach in fifteen minutes, swim for a bit, then we'll have lunch and wrap the paperwork up this afternoon. Or tomorrow, if we're having fun outside."

"But Mitch..."

Apparently Mitch wasn't taking no for an answer, because he stood and walked out of the conference room. Amy slipped her hair behind her ears and looked to Justin for help. He only shrugged and said, "I guess we're going for a dip in the ocean."

Great. Just great.

Thirty minutes later, Amy stood on the patio of Mitch's private beach with Justin. Justin wore his swim trunks and a tank top. She'd put on her bikini. And her cover up and her sunglasses and her sandals, determined to watch Justin and Mitch do whatever they wanted to in the water while she sat inside the cabana where she would sip tea and do some work.

Mitch approached, wearing his board shorts. Shirtless, he looked tanned, gorgeous and way too incredibly well muscled for a man in his forties. Amy swallowed as he stopped in front of her and frowned.

"Tell me that's not your laptop," Mitch said, motioning to the thick bag in her hand.

"Okay, it's not my laptop."

Mitch signaled for one of the attendants, who rushed over. "Take Ms. Parker's bag to my office and lock it up in the safe."

"Yes, Mr. Magruder." The attendant waited. Mitch arched a brow. Amy sighed and handed over her bag to the attendant, who rushed down the sidewalk toward the hotel.

"I said we're going to play in the water. That means all of us."

"Really, Mitch, I—"

"You going to take all that off or are we going to toss you in the ocean with your cover up and sandals on?"

Justin pulled off his shirt, showing off a broad expanse of shoulders, biceps and a well-defined chest and abdomen. Amy couldn't breathe surrounded by all this...testosterone.

Maybe the water would cool her off. And maybe they'd forget about her once she went in to take a swim. She kicked off her sandals and took off her sunglasses, then drew the cover up over her head. "Fine. I'm ready for a swim."

Mitch and Justin both stared at her. She supposed turnabout was fair. She'd ogled their bodies, too.

"Amy, you are gorgeous," Mitch said. "Why you hide a body like that under business suits is beyond my ability to understand."

Okay, now she was blushing. "Thanks." Honestly, she wasn't used to being looked at. She did hide her body. She was curvy. She had big boobs. She wanted to be appreciated for her mind, not breasts and hips and long legs.

"I'm going for a swim," she said, brushing past them and heading toward the water. Where if she was lucky, they wouldn't follow.

But they did. She felt them behind her. Watching her. Looking at her ass, no doubt.

For some strange reason, she no longer minded that they were looking.

The sand was hot. She hurried to the water's edge, relieved when the waves lapped at her feet and ankles. It was cold. She needed the cool water to knock some sense into her. As soon as she was in waist high, she dove in, letting the waves crash over her.

It was heaven. She swam out a few yards, loving the feel of the waves undulating under her. It was incredibly freeing, and oh so relaxing. She finally stopped, treading water and feeling for footing, landing on a sandbar. She stood in the water up to her breasts. Mitch swam up next to her and grinned as he stood up, shaking his head.

"Now that was refreshing," he said with a wide grin.

"Yes it was. I needed that."

She screamed when arms encircled her waist and swept her off her feet. Flailing about, she turned, realizing she was being held in Justin's arms.

"You scared the hell out of me," she said, splashing water in his face.

He shook his head and laughed. "Thought I was a shark, didn't you?"

"Maybe." All too aware of how good it felt to be nestled against his chest, she said, "You can put me down now."

One raven brow arched. "Oh, I don't think so." Instead, he bent a bit, then lifted her, clear out of the water, and she went sailing in the air, screaming at the top of her lungs. Instead of landing somewhere in the water, she was caught by another set of strong arms. This time, it was Mitch.

She glared at both of them. "You guys are not funny."

"We think we are," Mitch said, cradling her close, turning her toward him so her breasts were mashed against his chest. "You're safe with us, Amy. Don't worry."

She wasn't worried at all. Justin swam up and linked hands with Mitch underneath her, dropping her into the middle between them. She lay in their arms in the water, cradled against their chests while the two of them carried on a conversation about sports, seemingly ignoring her. It was a man hammock. She was comfortable, safe, and absolutely petrified. She was a sandwich in the middle of two amazingly desirable men.

Finally, she relaxed, letting her head rest against Justin's chest as they rocked her back and forth, the sound of their voices a constant comfort. She closed her eyes and let the sun bake her, the waves lapping over her skin.

She imagined the two of them taking her right there in the water, stripping off her top and each of them sucking a nipple into their greedy mouths, licking and biting until she writhed on top of the waves and begged them to fuck her. Her pussy clenched and she whimpered with need. Too long. She'd waited too long for an orgasm. Too long for a man. She craved strong, callused hands between her legs, searching her swollen slit and pumping fingers into her core, caressing her clit until she cried out in climax and demanded a hot cock to replace those fingers.

Maybe Santa would bring her *that* for Christmas. A nice fantasy come true in her stocking.

She smiled. Then felt the press of lips against hers.

Her eyes drifted open and Justin's face loomed in front of hers.

A million words hovered on her lips, all of them denial, every single one of them obliterated when his mouth came down on hers again, this time harder, hungrier. She gasped against him and his tongue slipped between her teeth, finding hers. It was an electric shock, a velvet fire as he licked her, his lips doing dangerous things to her senses. He dragged her upright. She bobbed in the water, her legs adrift, her arms clasping around his neck as he drove into her mouth with more intent.

She'd always known there was a primal side to Justin, this barely unleashed animal he kept tucked away in business suits. Now he was letting it out, letting her see it, and she couldn't get close enough to this side of him. She wanted more.

But another set of arms came around her, dragging her away from Justin. Justin smiled at her, nodded, and as she was turned she found Mitch in front of her, his hands slipping around her waist to draw her against him. Her heart slammed against her ribs, her mind nothing but liquid. She couldn't think this through.

"Don't," Mitch said. "Don't think about it. Just let it happen."

He laid her against his arm, and touched his lips to hers. Where Justin was all fiery passion, Mitch's kiss was softer, more coaxing and gentle, but still demanding that she pay attention. She was out of breath, and completely out of her mind.

Her world exploded as she realized that in the space of thirty seconds, she had been kissed by two different men. For someone who almost always lived in a man drought, this was overload to her senses. She felt Justin's presence behind her, his chest against her back, his lips pressed to her neck while Mitch continued to kiss her. As Justin's body pressed full against hers, she felt his cock—hard, insistent, rocking against her buttocks. Mitch's hard-on rested against her hip.

Oh, God. Fantasy was one thing, but this reality? She wasn't nearly ready for this. She palmed Mitch's chest and he broke the kiss. Justin backed away. Mitch grinned.

"I told you, Amy. You're safe with us. You don't need to worry." Mitch pushed off the bottom and swam to shore.

Shaken, Amy pushed back her hair and raised a trembling hand to her lips. She was almost afraid to turn around and look at Justin, afraid he'd mock her, accuse her. But she knew she'd have to face him sometime. She pivoted and he jerked her into his arms, his lips crashing into hers, still filled with the hunger that had consumed her with his first kiss.

She should pull away, regroup, gather her bearings. But God, she wanted him, had wanted him for a long time. She reached down, palmed his cock, shuddering at the rock hard feel of him against her hand. She wanted him inside her.

Justin dragged his lips away, leaned his forehead against

hers. "I could fuck you right here, Amy."

Her breasts felt heavy, her sex on fire with need. His words only inflamed her more.

"But not here. I want you alone. I don't want anyone else watching. Not right now." He took her hand and they walked out of the water. Every step was agony, seemingly taking forever to get to shore. Without a word they grabbed their things and headed back to the bungalows.

She thought that by the time they got back to the bungalows her ardor would be cooled.

Oh, no. It was worse. Walking alongside Justin—he'd held her hand the entire time—only made her want this more. She'd stopped questioning why. She knew why. The scene with Justin and Mitch in the water had just been a warm up. She didn't really understand why Mitch had left, and frankly, she didn't care. It had been fun kissing two men. Hot. Incredible. But she wanted Justin.

The realization was somewhat shocking. Though she didn't know why she was so surprised. Justin had been her fantasy man for a very long time. Maybe because she had never expected this to become a reality. And now it was going to be. It was really going to happen between them.

They reached the bungalows and Justin automatically went to her door, turning and waiting for her to get her key. Her hands were shaking—her hands were actually shaking! She couldn't believe it. She was no virgin. She'd had sex before. Quite a few times, in fact. But not for a while. And never with a man she'd wanted in the way she wanted Justin.

She handed him the key and he opened the door, holding it aside while she stepped in. He shut it, flipped the deadbolt, and didn't bother to turn on the light.

Amy set her bag on the table.

"I need a shower. Ocean salt. Makes me itchy."

Justin smiled and took her hand, led her to the bathroom and turned on the shower.

"Turn around."

She did, and he untied the string at her neck. She held onto the bikini top covering her breasts as he untied the laces at her back. Justin swept her hair to the side and pressed a kiss to the back of her neck. She shivered.

"Amy."

"Yes?"

"Let go, babe."

She wasn't sure if he was referring to her bikini top or the tension rocketing her body. She was nervous. God, she couldn't believe she was about to get naked with a coworker. If she thought about it too hard, she'd probably shut down completely.

She decided not to think about it at all. She let go of the top and Justin reached out, peeled the top away from her breasts. He inhaled.

"You're beautiful. I've thought about your breasts for years."

"Really."

"Yeah. Really. Wondering what they looked like under those crisp suits and blouses you hid them under." He swept his hands under her breasts. Oh, his hands felt so good. She'd been dying for him to touch her. She laid her head against his chest and just watched. He covered her breasts, reached for her nipples, using his thumbs to gently sweep over the buds. They tightened, her breasts swelling into his hands, her nipples sharp, aching points.

She could stay like this for hours, letting him touch her.

His hands were rough and she loved the feel of them playing over her sensitive nipples. He let go, and she whimpered. But then he moved in front of her, bent down, and reached for the ties at the sides of her bikini. He looked up at her, pulled the laces, and drew the material away.

She was naked. And then Justin looked at her pussy. His face was right there, his mouth so close. Her pussy quivered at the thought of what those full lips could do to her. She'd fantasized about it so many times, had made herself come thinking about him sucking her clit, sliding his tongue inside her, making her scream.

"I want to eat you until you come for me, Amy."

Her legs wobbled. She couldn't breathe normally. His breath warmed her sex. So close.

But then he stood, dropped his swim trunks. Amy swallowed. God, he was so perfect, just as she'd imagined. Amazingly well built, his cock erect and making her mouth water. He opened the shower door, stepped inside and held his hand out for her. She went in with him and he closed the door, drawing her under the spray.

"I figured we'd better get this shower out of the way or the water would get cold," he said.

Amy managed a shaky laugh. He was so right. She'd been lost in what he was doing, completely oblivious to the steamed up bathroom. She wet her hair and reached for the shampoo.

"Let me."

Surprised, she handed the shampoo to Justin, who poured some onto his hand. "Turn around."

She did, and Justin lathered her hair, massaging her scalp and neck. It, too, was a sensual experience. He didn't wash her hair like she did, doing it fast and perfunctory. He took his time, using his fingers in slow, circular movements. Oh, God the man had expert hands. She was melting. He moved her back and rinsed her hair, then poured conditioner on it. While she rinsed, he poured soap onto his hand, a wicked smile curving his lips.

"Turn around and place your hands against the wall," he instructed.

She palmed the wall and he placed his hands on her shoulders, sliding soap there and along her back, washing her, using the same slow motions he had used to wash her hair. He washed her entire body that way—her arms, her legs, reaching around to do her belly and breasts, but making sure to avoid her most sensitive areas until she was writhing under his hands, desperate for him to touch her. Then he pulled her under the spray and rinsed her.

She was throbbing all over, reaching for him, but he only smiled and placed a hand on her to hold her away. Instead, he poured more soap on his hands and washed himself, making her watch. And oh, did she ever enjoy watching him touch his own body. She finally had a chance to really look at him, from his well-defined arms, to the way his biceps flexed with every movement to his six pack abs that showed how hard he worked on his body. When he soaped his cock, stroking it back and forth, she leaned against the wall and licked her lips.

"I can't take much more of this, Justin," she said, not used to this kind of foreplay. She was accustomed to guys who got right down to business. This was torture.

He stepped under the water and rinsed his body, washed and rinsed his hair, then turned the shower off, grabbing a towel and wrapping it around her to dry her off. He dried her hair, then let her go grab a brush so she could brush out the tangles while he dried off.

She didn't take time to blow dry her hair. She didn't care.

This time she took the lead, grabbing Justin's hand and leading him out of the bathroom. But Justin wasn't having any of that. He swept her into his arms and carried her. She thought he was going to take her to bed.

He didn't. He took her to the back door, to the patio.

"Justin, it's the middle of the day." The sun was out, and though they were located on a private stretch of beach, someone could still walk by.

"I don't care. You look gorgeous in sunlight. I want to see you." He placed her down against the door. She leaned against the wall, the sunlight streaming across her body.

"Perfect," he said, then crouched down and spread her legs.

She palmed the wall, wishing she had something to hold onto.

"I told you, Amy. I'm going to eat you until you scream. I've been dying to hear you scream."

Chapter Five

Amy might scream right now. Her clit pulsed, her pussy clenched and she was wet. She was primed and ready and he hadn't even touched her yet.

Justin lowered his head and brushed his lips across the inside of her thigh. She shuddered out a moan.

"You smell so good. You always smell good. Edible." His tongue snaked out and licked along the seam of her pussy lips, making her quiver. He reached around and grasped her buttocks in his hands, tilting her upward, then planted his mouth over her.

Amy tangled her fingers in the wet strands of Justin's hair, holding onto him as he licked and sucked her clit. Hot, wet pleasure sizzled throughout her nerve endings, her whole body tense with need. She wasn't going to last. This had been building too long. Wetness trickled down her thighs—whether it was his saliva or her juices she couldn't tell, didn't care. She was wet, hot, wanted to come, wanted it now. She pumped her hips, driving her pussy into Justin's face.

He licked her up and down in slow, deliberate motions, then plunged his tongue inside her, lapping up the cream that spilled from her as she bucked and writhed against him. She pulled his hair, releasing a moan as she reached the very edge of endurance. When he slid two fingers inside her and then pressed his mouth over her clit and sucked, she was gone. She climaxed, her pussy gripping his fingers as the spasms racked her body in uncontrollable bursts of lightning.

Justin took her down easy, giving her time to catch her breath, keeping his fingers inside her and pumping them with slow movements. She finally remembered she was clutching his hair and let go, smoothing the strands with her fingers. He kissed her sex again, then stood, pressing against her, his mouth wet.

He leaned in, kissed her. He tasted like her—dear God that was hot—his tongue plunging inside her mouth like he was desperate for her. And she wanted him again. Just like that, she was needy all over again. She lifted her leg and wrapped it around his hip, feeling his cock heavy and hard against her belly. He lifted her, brought her to the bed and laid her down.

"I'll be right back," he whispered, slipping on his swim trunks. He was gone only a few minutes. When he came back, he had a few foil packets in his fingers and a wide grin on his face.

Amy leaned up on her elbows. "You didn't bring the whole box?"

"Voracious, are you?"

"I might be. There's been a drought."

"Here, too. We'll see who cries uncle first."

"It won't be me. I can guarantee it."

"I like a challenge," he said, waggling his brows.

"You would."

He slipped out of his shorts and tore open a packet, slipped on the condom, and crawled onto the bed, spreading her knees so he could climb between them.

She loved that things between them were so easy, so

lighthearted. She didn't know what she'd expected. Tension, maybe, like what they usually experienced when they worked together? It hadn't been like that since the moment they landed.

Maybe it was the air here in Hawaii. Maybe she finally relaxed. Maybe she was just ready for this and tired of dancing around the inevitable.

He pressed down on her, keeping his weight off but laying his body fully against hers. She loved the feel of his body against hers. There was so much she wanted to do with him, but not right now. She'd waited a long time for this.

"Fuck me, Justin."

His eyes went dark, and all sense of fun and laughter went out of them, replaced instead by that animalistic hunger that made her belly tumble. He grabbed her wrists and pulled them over her head, bending down to take one of her nipples into his mouth.

She arched her back, crying out when he sucked it hard between his tongue and the roof of his mouth. How did he know she needed more than just a light flick of tongue, a gentle caress? How could he seem to know her body so well? He suckled her nipple, teasing it with his tongue, his mouth, even nibbling her with his teeth until she wriggled uncontrollably underneath him. When he released her nipple, it stood upright and glistening, wet, and hard. He took the other in his mouth, conducting the same sweet torment until she begged him to stop, to fuck her.

He popped that nipple out of his mouth and nipped at her bottom lip. "You want my dick inside you, Amy?"

"Yes," she whispered, lifting her hips as if she could grab his cock and slip it inside her pussy.

"Do you know how long I've wanted to fuck you?"

"As long as I've thought about you fucking me. Now do it."

His mouth captured hers at the same time his cock found the entrance to her pussy and slid inside with one, sweet thrust.

No surprise, he fit her perfectly. He let go of her wrists so she could wrap her arms around him, her fingers roaming the hard planes of his flesh as he lifted and plunged inside her again. And again. Her walls tightened around him, gripping, raking her with pleasure each time he pulled out and drove into her with punishing force.

And she loved it, loved the way Justin powered his body inside her, gripped her buttocks to lift her so he could penetrate her deeper. He mastered her body, rubbing his pelvis against her clit, at the same time thrusting inside her and finding that special spot that sent her flying again. Her eyes wide open, she moaned his name, clutching his shoulders when he gave her yet another orgasm. And he watched her, just watched her, still pumping inside her and holding her close while she rode the wave, then slowed his pace, let her catch her breath.

But then he started in on her again, slowly at first, then picking up speed and voracity. Like a hurricane, he built the pressure until she couldn't take it anymore. This time, when she burst, he went with her, and he let her see the way his face tightened as he came, the way he gripped her shoulders and shuddered when he let loose a torrent of come and collapsed against her, burying his face in her neck.

Spent, she stroked his back while he played along her waist and hip. She waited for the awkwardness to set in, the moment when this fantastic experience became uncomfortable.

It didn't happen. Justin rolled to his side and took her with him, still inside her, waiting until he softened to pull out and dispose of the condom. Then he crawled back into bed and gathered her in his arms again, pulling her close and pressing his lips to hers.

She was drained. Happy. Apprehensive. Content.

Sleepy. Justin stroked her hair and she let her eyes drift shut, figuring she'd let worry set in later. Right now, she was going to fall asleep.

Justin woke with Amy in his arms. They'd slept a couple hours. She was still asleep.

Good.

He inhaled, let it out, stared at the ceiling and smiled. He couldn't have planned this better. Hell, he hadn't planned on this. Not all this...feeling. He'd wanted to show Amy a good time. He was pretty certain she'd had a good time. He hadn't counted on the gut punch of emotion that being with Amy had caused.

In the ocean, kissing her. Then with Mitch...goddamn, that had been hot. And Amy had been turned on. Really turned on. So had Mitch. He and Mitch hadn't even discussed Amy. They hadn't needed to. Mitch had just gone along, had sensed Amy's need. But Mitch knew what was what. He wasn't entrenched.

Was Justin?

Yeah. He was.

The big question though...was Amy?

She stirred in his arms, lifted her head, smiled. God, she was sexy, her hair disheveled from sleep, her lips swollen from his kisses.

"What time is it?"

"Four-thirty."

"Oh, God." She sat up, swept her hair back. "I never nap in the afternoon."

"You probably never get your brains fucked out in the afternoon, either."

She snorted. "No. That rarely happens."

Justin laced his fingers behind his head. "Rarely?"

She looked down at him. "Okay, never. I don't do this, Justin."

"I know. And whether you believe it or not, neither do I."

She blushed. He loved that about her. Didn't she know how special she was?

"So now what?" she asked.

"We have the rest of the day. We can do what we want."

"We need to finish signing the papers. What Mitch must think..."

"Mitch is probably off doing his own thing and happy not to be stuck in his office. Trying to corral him back in the office now would be impossible. We'll take it up in the morning. We can finish in an hour or less. The rest of the day is ours." He leaned up, grabbed Amy and pulled her on top of him. Her breasts pillowed against his chest, her legs aligned with his. He liked how she felt, loved putting his hands on her. He threaded his fingers through her hair and pulled her face toward his, kissed her, slow and gentle at first.

No hesitation on her part. She opened for him willingly, sliding her body against him. Like satin, she glided over him, her belly cradling his quickly hardening cock. She moaned against his mouth, rocked her hip against his dick, massaging him, making him crazy.

She pushed off with her hands and lifted, smiling down at him. Her teeth captured her bottom lip and her eyes...so sexy when they were half-lidded like that.

She kissed his jaw, moving over his neck and lower, to his

shoulders, climbing down his body and nipping at him with her teeth. He tossed his head back on the pillow and just watched as she tasted his skin. Rock hard now, his balls drew up tight against his body. Her hair was splayed out across his skin as she maneuvered her way across his chest, pausing to lick his nipples, bite at them, tease him.

"Christ, Amy." The sensation shot straight to his cock. He reached for her, but she brushed him away and continued south, kissing the planes of his abdomen, sweeping her hands down over his thighs, disregarding his throbbing dick that begged for her attention as she moved down his body.

Her face was aligned with his crotch now, and she looked up at him, smiled, then wrapped her hand around the base of his cock, sliding upward in a spiraling motion that rocketed his hips off the bed. He drove into her hand, fucking the soft satin of her palm. She squeezed him as she neared the tip, rewarded with a pearly drop of liquid from his cockhead. She bent over and licked it away with the flat of her tongue.

His hips jerked up, propelling his cock against that warm, wet velvet. He could come right now from that one lick. But he wanted more. A lot more. He grabbed a handful of her hair and wrapped it around his fist, holding tight while she surrounded the crest and sucked, grazed it with her teeth, then took his cock fully into her mouth inch by inch.

He didn't know what was hotter—watching what she was doing or being able to feel each sensation. She really seemed to love licking and sucking him, from the tip of his cock all the way down to his ball sac. It made him insane when she dragged her tongue over his balls, then below to the sensitive ridge underneath. She explored every inch of him, then devoured his shaft until it disappeared in the warm recesses of her mouth. He pumped upward, letting her take as much as she could. She never balked, gripping the base of his cock and stroking him as she sucked.

He was going to go off in her mouth and that's not what he wanted. He wanted to be buried inside her. He pulled her hair, releasing his cock from between her lips, then dragged her upward.

"Fuck my dick, baby," he whispered, his voice hoarse with need.

Amy smiled, her mouth wet, and she leaned over and grabbed a foil packet, tearing it open. She put his condom on, taking her damn sweet time, too. He gritted his teeth as she slid the condom over his aching cock, then straddled him. He had a bird's eye view of her sweet pussy lips hovering right over the top of his dick. She paused, leveled a killer look at him that reduced him to ash, then mounted him inch by torturous inch.

Justin gripped the bed sheets, trying not to groan as she surrounded him with gripping heat. He was already on the edge. Amy wasn't making this any easier. Her breasts spilled forward and he captured them with his hands, pulling on her nipples until they stood prominent and hard. She gasped as he tugged them, tilted her head back and held her breasts out for him to fondle. At the same time, she ground her pussy against him until he saw stars, his balls tightening, filling with the come he was eager to shoot.

No, not ready yet. He wanted more of this. He pulled her forward, bringing her chest against his, dragging her lips to his for a hard, hot kiss. He roamed her back with his hands, sweeping against the fine sheen of sweat coating her skin, knowing she was working for this just as he was. He grasped her buttocks, loving the feel of the firm globes in his hands, the way she bounced on top of him, rocking against him as she took her fill of his dick.

When he spread her cheeks and probed the soft crack

between, she gasped, stilled, and began to pant.

Oh, yeah. She liked having her anus touched. He could tell from the way her pussy clenched, spasmed around him. He rubbed his finger outside the hole, teasing her as he lifted his cock and buried it deeper inside her. Her moans, the way she shifted against him, told him what she liked.

When he slid his fingertip inside her anus, she cried out, clenching his shoulders, her pussy gripping him in a trembling vise. Her juices poured over his thighs.

"You like it in the ass, Amy?" he asked, shoving his finger in deeper while shoveling his cock in and out of her. "Do you like the thought of being double fucked?"

She didn't answer, just panted, whimpered, and dragged her nails across his skin. He slid his finger in further, burying it all the way, and she cried out, bucking against him as she came with a wild shudder.

Fuck. He couldn't take anymore. He pumped hard and fast, feeling his own orgasm rip through him. He thrust repeatedly against her, riding out one hell of a climax until he was empty and out of breath.

He continued to hold her, just like that, not wanting to let go of her. Finally, she climbed off and they went into the bathroom to clean up, both of them quiet. Amy fixed them drinks and they sat naked on the chairs in the living room. He liked that she wasn't modest. He mostly enjoyed looking at her naked.

He really liked that she'd enjoyed his finger in her ass. It made him wonder what else she'd enjoy. But he didn't want to push her, didn't want her to think this was all about sex.

"How about we get dressed and go get something to eat? I don't know about you, but you've fucked me into near starvation," he said.

She laughed. "Sounds good to me. I'm hungry, too."

Justin went next door and changed, and came back to pick up Amy. She'd put on a short skirt and a halter, her hair pulled back in a ponytail. Damn, his cock twitched just looking at her. As much as the business Amy turned him on, this carefree, sexy side of her made him even hotter.

"It's nice to see you relaxed," he said when they were seated in a nice, dark both at a trendy little beach restaurant.

"Actually, this is quite a departure for me."

"Yeah. I know. I see you almost every day. Sometimes even on weekends. I probably know you as well as any of your friends," he said, pouring wine for them both.

"That's true. I don't have that many friends anyway."

"Why's that?"

"Who has time? The friends I do have are busy building families. They have husbands, children. I haven't...gotten there yet," she said, staring into her wine glass.

"Do you want to?"

She looked up at him. "Yes. I guess so. I don't know. I'm thirty-three and I just don't know yet."

Justin shrugged. "You don't need kids to complete your life, Amy. There's no official roadmap, you know."

"Tell that to my parents. They're livid I don't have a husband and family yet. On more than one occasion they've had the gay talk with me."

Justin nearly choked on his wine. "The gay talk?"

"Yes. The 'we'll still love you even if you're a lesbian' talk. I was mortified."

"You're kidding."

"I only wish I was. I mean, it's great they're so open

minded. If I was gay, I'd have the best parents in the world. But I'm not. I've been focusing on my career, not my personal life. They just don't get that. They think there's something wrong with me."

Justin smirked. "Most parents don't. Mine thought I should find a girl and settle down right out of college."

"See? So yours pressure you too?"

"Yeah. And the whole idea of me traveling around and interning while in college was unacceptable to them. Especially when I hooked up with Mitch. They thought he was a bad influence."

Amy lifted her glass, took a sip. "Was he?"

"Probably."

She laughed. "He seems to have done quite well for himself."

"He wanted me to work for him after college. We hit it off really well."

"Why didn't you?"

"Because we were close friends, and I didn't want any favors when I started out. I wanted to do it on my own. Make sense?"

"Yes. It does."

She was studying him. He wondered what she was thinking. Or maybe he already knew. "I'm not using you, or sex with you, to advance my position at the firm, Amy."

"I wasn't thinking that."

"Yes you were. It's no secret there's been a competitive animosity between us for years."

She nodded. "It's true. We didn't start out on the right foot."

"You feel threatened by me."

"I do not. I just find your tactics aggressive and over the top."

"We don't approach bringing in clients in the same way. It doesn't mean my method is wrong. It works, doesn't it?"

She glared across the table at him. "It does work. But it borders on unethical."

He snorted. "Just because it isn't your way doesn't mean it's the wrong way." He grasped her hand. She snatched it back.

He grinned. "It makes my dick hard when you get all high and mighty like that."

Her eyes widened, then narrowed. "Are you playing with me?"

"Not yet, but I'd like to. I didn't know you liked it in public, Amy. How kinky."

She rolled her eyes. "Justin, I don't know what to make of you."

He held up his hands. "What you see is what you get. I won't lie to you. Ever. Amy, I've wanted you since the moment I walked into the firm."

"Yeah, right. I didn't like you at all."

"Is that the truth?"

She paused. "You're five years younger than me. You were a kid when you first started."

"Honey, I wasn't a kid then and I'm not now. Or haven't you figured that out yet?"

Her eyes went smoky. "Yeah, you're definitely all man. But this isn't going to work between us."

"Why not?"

"Age difference. We work together. Those two alone spell

disaster."

"It would work if we make it work. You're just reaching for excuses." And he wasn't going to let it happen. Now that he had her, he wasn't going to allow her to walk away.

"What do you want from me, Justin?"

Now it was his turn to pause. He wanted her full attention.

"Everything, Amy. I want it all."

Amy stared at her laptop, trying to get the brief written, but it wouldn't cooperate.

Justin had wanted to come into her room after they'd finished dinner. He'd wanted to take her to a club. He'd wanted to do a lot of things. With her. She'd said no to everything, claiming she needed to get a little work done because she was behind schedule.

That much was true. She had a brief to write, her schedule to update. She wanted to go over Mitch's paperwork—the rest of it—one last time before they finished it all tomorrow, since she'd been utterly distracted this morning.

Bad news—she was still distracted—her dinner conversation with Justin occupying her mind this time. Which was the main reason she'd begged off spending any more of the evening with him.

She needed some distance, some time to think about what had happened between them.

What she'd done was irreversible. She'd slept with a coworker. He'd never take her seriously now. She knew that no matter what Justin said, he was ambitious. He wanted a senior partnership at the firm, and she knew he would let nothing get in his way.

Especially her. Which meant he was going to use sex as a

stepping stone. Whether that was thinking he could warm her up as a way to gain access to the partnership, or blackmailing her into advancing, she didn't know.

Being with him had been fun...oh God it had been more than fun. It had been everything she could have imagined, and more. Justin was an incredible lover. Considerate, passionate and making sure her needs were taken care of.

She wanted more. A lot more. But that wasn't going to happen. She had to forget about it and hope to God things could go back to the way they were before.

The problem was, she couldn't stop thinking about him. About the two of them together. They fit so well. Not only sexually, but in other ways, too. Both driven, competitive, their backgrounds were even similar. They made a good pair.

Too bad it was never going to be. She simply wouldn't allow it. It would be a dangerous career move, and her career was everything. She'd spent the past fifteen years thinking of nothing *but* her career. She'd sacrificed. She wasn't going to throw it all away now simply because Justin was good in bed.

Oh, man was he ever good in bed.

Stop it, Amy. Work.

She focused on her laptop and the brief outlined in front of her.

But it wasn't at all what she had on her mind.

Chapter Six

Amy was already in Mitch's boardroom the next morning at the designated time. She hadn't waited for Justin, and the look on his face when he walked into the conference room told her he was irritated.

She always knew when he was mad. His jaw clenched tight and he barely spoke.

Yes, she'd deliberately avoided him. She'd eaten breakfast in one of the hotel restaurants, then wandered around outside until it was time for their meeting. And she knew Justin would come to her door in the morning wanting to have breakfast. Or maybe more than that.

Too bad. He was going to have to get used to business as usual, because that's the way things were going to be from now on. They'd had their fun, but after yet another sleepless night, Amy had come to the realization that she couldn't possibly jeopardize her future on an affair. And that's all she and Justin could ever have—an affair.

What else could they have—a relationship? The firm would never allow it, which meant that either one of them, or both, would lose their jobs. She'd worked too damn hard to walk away now, and she knew Justin wouldn't either. That left a stalemate. Best to end things now before they got too involved.

At least the air conditioning was working in the conference room today. Because looking at Justin made her hot. And she'd dressed appropriately this time. Sleeveless top, no jacket, and a cotton skirt. Casual. Comfortable. And a good, sturdy bra that would reveal no traitorous nipples.

"Good morning," she said to Justin as he slid his briefcase across the table.

"Morning." He went for the coffee. Didn't even look at her.

She felt a twinge in her stomach, but brushed it aside. She had nothing to feel guilty about.

Amy busied herself with the paperwork, setting them up where they'd left off yesterday so they'd be ready to dive in as soon as Mitch arrived. It was Christmas Eve. If they were lucky, they could wrap this up and catch a commercial flight home. Not that she had anything to do. Her family was on a ski trip in Vail and she wasn't the least bit interested in skiing over the holidays. She intended to catch up on work. But spending Christmas in Hawaii? With Justin? Too—romantic, which meant risky. No thanks. She'd rather jingle her bells alone and watch reruns of *It's a Wonderful Life* and *A Christmas Story* and a few of her other favorites on television. She'd call her family on Christmas Day which would take care of the familial obligations. Then she'd dig into more work. By the day after, she'd be ready to head back to the office, the entire messy holiday thing behind her.

Ho, ho, ho. Or maybe she was humbug. Whatever.

"Maybe we'll finish up early today and can catch a flight," she said to Justin.

"Can't wait to get away from me?" he asked. "Was it so bad, Amy, that you need to run?"

"No. No, it's not like that. Justin, please."

"Forget it. I thought you were an adult, Amy. I was wrong. I thought you could handle this—us—that maybe...forget it." He grabbed one of the portfolios and pulled it in front of him, flicking open his pen.

Never mind what? What was he going to say? "Justin, what—"

"Morning, everyone."

She had no chance to probe further because Mitch walked in.

"Good morning, Mitch," she said, turning her gaze to the reason for their being in Hawaii. Focus. She had to remember that, though her heart was pounding and it had nothing to do with finalizing the deal on the table.

"Ready to get this one in the bag, Amy?"

She gave Mitch her brightest smile. "You know it. This shouldn't take long. We had almost finished up yesterday."

Mitch pulled up a chair and opened the portfolio. "Right. Yesterday. Before playtime. Always have to find time to play, Amy." He leaned across the table and captured the tendril of hair she'd left loose today, dragging it through his fingers. "You have a gorgeous mouth."

The air was sucked out of the room as Mitch reminded her what had happened between the two of them yesterday. Or the three of them. In the ocean. The kisses.

"Mitch. Business."

"You can have both, Amy. Quit worrying. The merger isn't in any jeopardy."

Her breath caught, held, until he let loose of the curl he'd held in his hand, then resumed studying the paperwork in front of him. Amy's gaze shot to Justin. She expected to see anger. All she saw was...interest. And then he, too, dropped his gaze to the acquisition papers, leaving her alone with her confused thoughts, none of which had anything to do with business, and everything to do with the two men occupying the room with her.

"As usual, you two have done a fine job. You negotiated all the changes I requested, and the financial aspect looks fine." Mitch signed the last page of the paperwork and handed the three copies over to Amy. "We're done."

"Congratulations, Mitch," Justin said. "Amacor Sports is a fine company and they'll do right by yours and your people."

"I know they will. You did a good job brokering the deal. And now that's one less worry for me. And a lot more capital to invest in other fun projects." Mitch leaned back in the chair while Amy and Justin filed the paperwork away in their briefcases.

Amy blew out a breath, thankful that was over with. It had taken a little longer than expected, mainly because Mitch had to break a couple times for telephone calls. But it was finally done. She glanced at her watch. "Mitch, can I get your secretary to check flights for me?"

Mitch frowned. "Flights? Why?"

"I thought I'd catch an early one out."

"You have plans with your family for Christmas?"

"Oh. No. They're all in Vail. I don't ski."

"Boyfriend?"

She laughed. "No. Just me and some classic television and a bit of work to catch up on."

"Amy, it's Christmas Eve. You're not spending it alone." Mitch turned to Justin. "Were you flying back today?"

Justin shook his head. "Hell no. Christmas in Hawaii? I wouldn't miss it."

"Good. Then it's settled. We just secured this deal and I'm

in the mood to celebrate. Amy, go change. We're going out on the boat. Meet me downstairs in a half hour."

Oh, no. "Mitch, really."

"Do you want me to call David and tell him that one of his junior partners wasn't placating his biggest client?"

Shit. "But that's blackmail, Mitch."

Mitch grinned. "So it is. Half hour?"

She shook her head. "Half hour."

Boat? The one-hundred-and-twenty-foot beast was no boat. Yacht, definitely. And a true beauty. Sleek as one of the most beautiful dolphins she'd ever seen. Blue and white and it cut through the water like it was sailing on glass.

Amy stood at the bow and let the wind whip through her hair, the salt of the ocean stinging her face and the fresh breeze cooling her sun-warmed skin.

Truthfully, she was glad she came. Mitch's yacht had every amenity, from food to drinks to music and servants catering to her every whim. There was even a spa room and she was told she'd be having a massage later so she could unwind. Mitch's orders.

Yeah, she needed to unwind all right. But right now she was simply enjoying being out on the water.

"Miss?"

She whipped around at the strange voice. A smiling crew member held a tray of drinks in his hands. She gave him a suspicious glare.

"Is there alcohol in this?"

"No, ma'am. This is tea. Raspberry on your left, and regular on your right."

She giggled. "Sorry. I had a bad run in with a Mai Tai the other evening."

The man laughed. "My wife can't handle those either. They pack a hard punch."

"You're telling me." She selected a raspberry tea, thanked the servant and leaned against the railing, enjoying the way the yacht effortlessly skated through the water.

Justin and Mitch were at one of the tables, having cocktails and smoking cigars. And laughing. Amy couldn't bring herself to join them. She felt guilty.

No, that wasn't quite right. She felt like a wretched, awful bitch and she'd treated Justin like shit. And he hadn't deserved it. Just because she had no intentions of starting up a relationship with him didn't mean she should discard him like yesterday's newspaper. She owed him an apology. And apologizing to Justin was something Amy hadn't done before.

She took a long swallow of tea and maneuvered her way toward their table, stopping between them. Justin gazed at her, his eyes hidden behind smoky dark sunglasses.

"Hey," he said.

"Hey yourself."

"Enjoying the water, Amy?" Mitch asked.

"It's heaven on earth, Mitch. Thank you for making me stay." She turned again toward Justin, swallowed hard and said, "I'm sorry."

Justin smiled and reached an arm up to slide around her waist.

And just like that, she was forgiven.

Wow. She didn't deserve for it to be that easy. She so didn't understand men. And Justin rubbed her lower back while seemingly ignoring her, which made her chew her bottom lip.

Did she want his attention? Hadn't she spent the past twenty-four hours trying to figure out a way *not* to get his attention?

"I think I'll go get that massage now," she said, backing up a step. "Enjoy your drinks."

"Enjoy your massage," Mitch said with a grin.

"I intend to." She needed it. She was wound up tighter than a violin string.

The spa was part of the gym, which was quite expansive, with state of the art equipment, including a sauna and whirlpool and separate showers for Mitch's guests. Amy was greeted by a smiling woman who directed her where to change into one of the fluffy bathrobes, then escorted her into the room where a petite young woman named Collette was waiting to give her a massage.

Collette was mercifully quiet and concentrated on massaging the kinks out of Amy's tight muscles. Thank God she wasn't one of those masseuses who talked your ear off. That would have only made Amy more tense.

She started with Amy on her back, working her fingers into Amy's scalp, then temples and down into her neck before moving onto her arms and fingers. It was heaven and Amy felt the tension drain from her body. By the time Collette moved down to her legs, Amy was half asleep.

"You must turn over now, miss," Collette whispered near her ear.

Amy stretched and Collette held up the towel while she flipped over onto her stomach, her face down in the little hole in the massage table. She closed her eyes and shut out the world along with it.

Oh, yeah. This was heaven. Collette's strong fingers started working on the backs of her arms, then up to her neck.

"Excuse me, miss. I'll be right back."

"Mmmm, hmmmm." Amy didn't care if it took her a half hour. Just lying here with the soft music playing in the cool, candlelit private room was absolutely perfect.

Collette returned quietly. Amy hadn't even heard the door close. She might have even dozed off. She heard Collette rub her hands together, no doubt having poured more of that delicious scented oil on her hands, and then started working on her shoulders.

Oh, that was so good. Her touch was firmer now, rougher, digging deeper into her muscles. But slower. It was almost a sensual massage, the kind of caress a lover would—

Amy lifted her head, turned it over her shoulder.

Justin was in the room, not Collette. Smiling down at her as he moved his hands over her back. Her sex clenched, her clit trembling with the force of her attraction to him.

"Justin, what are you—"

"Lay back down and let me massage you."

His cock was hard, outlined against his shorts. She wanted to reach out and massage him, too, but she did as he asked and resumed her position face down on the table, anticipation making her tremble.

So much for her resolve. Did she have *any* willpower around him?

He worked that tight spot between her neck and shoulder blades where her tension always seemed to settle. His hands were strong, his fingers firm and he had no reluctance about digging deep into her muscles, melting away each knot until she groaned with utter pleasure.

He had great hands.

"It makes my dick hard when you moan like that," he said,

continuing to minister to her back.

"Does it now?" Her sex tingled.

"Yeah." He moved to her lower back, using his thumbs now and swirling in a circular motion. When he poured more oil on his hands and let them slide over her rear, she arched her hips up, wanting more. He squeezed her flesh and she whimpered, wanting his fingers elsewhere.

"Justin."

"Yeah, babe."

"Please." Her body was so sensitized to his touch, so needy for him that she wasn't above begging.

"Shh. I know what you need. Just relax." He poured oil right onto her skin. It trickled down the crack of her ass, onto her pussy, and she quivered at the sensual contact. When he followed it with his fingers, she shuddered, spreading her legs wide to give him access.

"Yes. That's it," she whispered, lifting against his hand. When she started to turn, he pressed his palm flat against her lower back.

"Stay there."

She raised her head and looked at him. "I can't touch you this way."

"This isn't about me. Now lay your head down and concentrate on what I'm doing."

She did, and he rewarded her by cupping her pussy, sliding his oil-slickened hand over her throbbing sex. Rubbing her like this, forcing her to focus only on the movements of his hand around her clit and pussy lips soon had her writhing against his hand. She felt engorged, and utterly desperate to release the physical and emotional anxiety that had wrapped around her for so long.

But he teased her—he was so good at it—seeming to know when she hung right on the top of the wave, and refusing to let her crash. And each time he brought her closer and closer, only to move his fingers away from the sweet spot.

By now she was panting, gripping the edge of the table in desperate attempt to drive her clit against his hand and make herself come. But he knew it and he was in charge here, not her. She wanted to say she enjoyed the ride, but she clung to the edge of sanity, frantic for the searing wet heat that awaited her, that only this man could give her.

"Goddamnit, Justin." She'd had enough. She lifted, but he used his hand to hold her down again, and this time he cupped her pussy, dragged his thumb over her clit in very deliberate motions, and didn't stop.

She climaxed in great, heaping waves, crying out and not caring who heard it. She'd been denied too long and she deserved this release. She intended to take every loud second of it and then some. When the ripples had died down to trickles, she breathed a satisfied sigh and relaxed, completely spent.

Justin pressed a kiss to her shoulder. "When you come...you really come."

She turned her head to the side and smiled. "You made me work for it."

"You're nothing if not tenacious about something you want bad, Amy."

He knew her so well. "What am I going to do about you?" she wondered aloud.

"I have a list of about forty-five things."

She snorted and sat up, then swung her legs over the side of the table. "I can think of one thing that's probably number one on your list." She directed her gaze to his cock, now tenting quite prominently against his shorts. She leaned over to reach for him, but he grabbed her hands, pulled her upright and kissed her knuckles.

"I told you, Amy. This wasn't about me. It was about you."

"But Justin, you're—"

"Hard?" He smiled. "Yeah. I'll live."

"I can take care of that."

"Don't I know it. We'll talk about that later. You're relaxed and content. Let's leave it at that."

He leaned into her, pulled her into his arms and kissed her. Not a passionate kiss, but one with feeling, with emotion behind it. It left Amy surprised, and profoundly confused. When he pulled back, making sure to put distance between them, she slipped an errant hair behind her ear and fumbled for a topic. "I suppose Collette is off gossiping about the hot sex one of Mitch's guests is currently enjoying in the massage room."

Justin leaned against the wall. "Mitch pays his employees extremely well. I doubt they say a word about anything to anyone. No one would want to lose a job working for him. And discretion is mandatory if you're employed in his upper realm."

"Good to know." She shrugged into her robe and stood. "Where is Mitch?"

"He was on the phone when I left him."

"Speaking of someone who needs to take a day off..."

Justin laughed. "Yeah. He takes plenty of time off, but he still always works."

"You know him pretty well."

"Well enough. We spent a lot of off hours together when I interned with him, and I've continued to hang out with him through the years."

"You like him a lot."

"Yeah. We're good friends. He never treated me like a kid, even when I was one. I respect that about him."

Amy could understand that appeal, especially for someone like Justin. Brilliant, up and coming, years ahead of the curve, but always younger than his peers. It had to irritate. Amy was probably one of the biggest offenders there. She had judged him on his age instead of his skills.

"I'm sorry."

"For what?" he asked, brows knitted.

"For doing exactly what you hated most. For treating you like you were too young to be as good as you were."

He shrugged and grinned. "It's okay. Everyone has to prove themselves, not just talk about how good they are."

She smiled, remembering what he was like when he first came to the firm. "You did plenty of talking."

"Yeah, I did, didn't I?"

"But you also delivered on every promise. And I was jealous as hell."

"The great Amy Parker, jealous? Please. You had me running in circles just to keep up with you. I've never faced a more formidable opponent."

She blushed under his compliment. "Now you're full of shit."

"I never lie, Amy. I worked twice as hard to be half as good as you."

Was that a line, or was it the truth? She searched his face, but found nothing there that would lead her to believe he was telling her anything but the honest truth.

"Thank you. Coming from you, that's an incredible compliment. You've been breathing down my neck since your first day at the firm. I keep waiting for you to pass me by."

"We're both good at what we do. That's why we're so well matched."

"I guess so." Justin, man of never ending surprises.

"How about we go drag Mitch off the phone and see if he wants to do some fishing before we head back to shore?"

"That sounds great."

Chapter Seven

After fishing and then eating, they'd spent the better part of the day out on Mitch's yacht lying around in the sun and talking. And Justin could tell Amy had had a wonderful time. She'd forgotten about work, about flying home, about everything except enjoying herself.

Exactly what he'd wanted for her.

And the massage hadn't hurt any, either. Making her come had sure seemed to improve her mood in a major way. She'd been smiling, laughing and much more relaxed since then.

While his balls had stayed in a knot and he'd suffered a perpetual hard-on the entire time.

Erections built character, right? Or something stupidly philosophical like that. All he knew was it hurt like hell and his mind was singly focused on sinking inside Amy's hot pussy and relieving the ache that plagued him all over.

After they disembarked, Amy had excused herself to take a shower, especially after Mitch had insisted they come to his place to spend Christmas Eve with him tonight. Since they had nothing else to do, they had agreed. With Amy gone, it had given Justin time to meet with Mitch and make a suggestion. A really personal, intimate suggestion.

Mitch had raised his brows, asked if Justin was certain that's what he wanted, and more importantly, what Amy wanted. Justin wasn't a hundred percent sure what Amy wanted, but he wanted to offer her a Christmas gift she'd never forget. And if she was game, then it was on.

He and Mitch had shared women before. It was no big deal. Until now. Because Justin was in love with Amy. Even Mitch knew that. But this was a once in a lifetime experience for Amy, something she'd fantasized about. And he wanted her to have it.

Once. After that, he intended to tell her how he felt, and that he didn't intend to ever share her again. After that, the ball would be in her court and the decision up to her.

He hoped things would go his way. But he wasn't in charge of Amy's heart.

After taking a shower, he put on a pair of black pants and a black and red flowered Hawaiian shirt to get in the spirit of both the islands and the holiday. He slipped on a pair of shoes and went to knock on Amy's door. She opened it.

"Wow. You're gorgeous."

"Thank you. So are you. Great shirt."

A week ago she'd never have said that about a funky shirt like this. And she was gorgeous in a red body-hugging dress and sandals. She'd gotten into the spirit too, with a hibiscus in her hair, tucked behind her ear. He leaned in and pressed a soft but lingering kiss to the side of her lips.

"You ready for a special night?"

She tilted her head to the side. "I guess so. I'm not much for Christmas. My family doesn't do presents. They just fly off and ski."

"You've missed out," he said, holding the door open for her. "I guess I'll have to come up with a special gift for you."

She quirked a brow, then walked out the door.

They walked over to Mitch's private cottage overlooking the

beach, all glass and modern angles. Justin held Amy's arm as she maneuvered the back steps and bypassed the pool and spa. He didn't bother knocking on the back door, just punched in the security code and slid open the door.

"You and Mitch must be close if he gave you the code," Amy said as they stepped into Mitch's living room.

"He trusts me," Justin said with a wink. "Hey, Mitch. We're here!"

"Be right down," Mitch said from the top of the curving staircase.

"This place is gorgeous," Amy remarked. "I've never been in here. Modern, yet very comfortable."

"Yeah, Mitch likes it to look lived in." From the comfortable cloth-covered sofas to the rugs spread all over the polished tile floor, it made people feel welcome. Justin always felt like he could slip off his shoes and put his feet up. At some rich peoples' homes he was afraid to even move, let alone sit down.

Mitch came downstairs, looking casual as always in khaki pants and a polo shirt. And a Santa hat.

"Cute," Amy said, her lips curving.

Mitch moved to the bar. "Ho, ho, ho. Gotta get into the spirit. And speaking of...spirits?"

Justin went to the bar and pulled out a stool for Amy. She slid onto it, giving him a glimpse of upper thigh. Mitch noticed, too.

"What would you like, Amy?"

"It's Christmas Eve, Mitch. I'll leave it up to you."

Mitch arched a brow. "That could be dangerous."

"I'll live dangerously tonight then."

The air in the room crackled with tension. Did Amy have any idea what was up? He hoped so. He hoped she wanted what he wanted to give her.

Mitch fixed drinks and handed them out. Amy took a sip, then another. "Oh. This is really good. What's in it?"

"You don't want to know," Mitch said.

"Okay, then," she replied with a tilt of the glass in his direction.

Whatever was in it, there was a ton of alcohol. Justin shook his head at Mitch. "Are you trying to get my lady drunk?"

Amy's gaze shot to Justin. He waited for denial. All he saw was warmth and the hint of a smile.

"Maybe I am," Mitch said. "What happens when you get drunk, Amy?"

"I lose my inhibitions."

"Then drink up."

She laughed. "You're a bad boy, Mitch."

"You don't know the half of it, Amy."

"Maybe I'd like to."

This was interesting. Justin moved in closer to Amy, his hip brushing her shoulder. She leaned alongside him without hesitation, her hair tickling his arm as she rubbed her head against his arm.

Was she trying to tell him something? He tested his theory by wrapping his arm around her shoulder, lazily tracing her collarbone with his fingertips. Mitch watched intently. Amy watched Mitch, yet didn't try to move Justin's questing fingers as they crept lower, closer to the swell of Amy's breast.

Justin's cock began to swell, too, and he exchanged glances with Mitch. Mitch's gaze was heated and he didn't seem to want to spend time looking at Justin. His attention shot back to Amy, to Justin's fingers tracing a pattern over Amy's right breast.

"Do you like that, Amy?" Mitch asked, looking casual and relaxed as he sipped his drink and watched.

"Yes."

"Does it bother you that I'm watching?"

"No, Mitch. It doesn't."

"Would you mind if I came over there?"

Amy paused. This was it, Justin thought. Decision time.

Amy tilted her head back and regarded Justin, indecision clear in her beautiful eyes.

"Justin, I—"

"I know what you want, babe."

She frowned. "I don't understand."

"You want us both, don't you?"

Amy's breath caught, held, her heart in her throat.

You want us both. Justin had said the words, had voiced her naughtiest fantasy. How was she supposed to answer that?

With the truth. She'd waited a lifetime for this, and she was seconds from being able to have it. But her feelings for Justin were different than they were for Mitch.

She was confused.

"We'll sort us out later. Tonight is just for you. I want this for you," Justin said. "I want to give this to you."

"You planned this." He knew. Somehow, he knew.

"Yes. To a certain extent. It's obvious you're attracted to Mitch."

"And you're okay with that?" Was she okay with it? With Justin being so willing to share her after what she and Justin had done? Her mind whirled with the possibilities.

And suddenly, Mitch was right there next to her, his hand resting above her left knee.

"I think the two of you have some personal relationship issues to sort out," Mitch said, sweeping her hair over her shoulder. "But not tonight. Tonight is for fun. Just the three of us."

The three of us. Dear God, could she?

She looked down where Mitch's hand rested on her leg. "Mitch, you're a client."

"Not tonight, Amy. Tonight, I'm a man who finds you incredibly desirable. Tonight, Amy, you're fired."

She sucked in a breath, certain the room was spinning. Her mind was awash with thoughts—too many to sort through.

"Maybe it's time to stop thinking and just enjoy," Justin said, licking the sensitive spot just underneath her earlobe. "Maybe it's time to give yourself a Christmas gift—two men to unwrap, Amy."

She shuddered at the thought. Two men. Just for her.

What the hell was she waiting for? She'd never have another moment like this. She'd be insane to pass it up.

She tilted her head back to look at Justin while she placed her hand over Mitch's.

"Yes."

Justin leaned in and took her mouth, kissing her with a passion that took the last of her breath. At the same time, Mitch's hand moved up her leg, creeping toward her thigh. He leaned in, the warmth of his breath caressing her neck. When his lips pressed against her throat, she shuddered at the sensation of being cocooned between the two of them. Neither one of them crowded her, pushed her too fast. Instead, they...worshipped her, with slow, deliberate kisses meant to drug her, to turn her on, to bring her pleasure.

She was going crazy, her mind going off like sparklers on the Fourth of July as she tried to process what was happening. Instead of two hands on her body, there were four. Instead of one set of lips, there were two. On her mouth, her neck, her shoulder, the swell of her breasts. Hands moved to the straps of her dress, dragging them down her shoulders and arms. They stood her up and moved her into the living room—to the sofa, she thought, she really wasn't sure because someone was kissing her while she was led into the other room. They swapped, first Justin's mouth on her, and then Mitch would drag her into his arms and press his lips to hers.

She didn't need alcohol. She was drunk on sensual kisses, languorous caresses to every part of her exposed skin. They stood her between them and she felt the tug of her zipper. She was facing Mitch now as Justin pulled her dress down, baring her breasts to Mitch.

In all her ménage fantasies, she thought she'd be embarrassed to be laid bare in front of two men. Instead, she felt exhilarated, empowered, like a goddess undressing for her subjects. Men who were about to pleasure her—because tonight, it really was all about her. And she reveled in it with unashamed abandon, didn't care that she felt selfish about it. This was only going to happen once and she intended to make the most of it.

"You are so beautiful," Mitch said, reaching out to trace his fingers over her breasts. Her nipples puckered as he circled her areolas, then cupped her breasts and skimmed her nipples with his thumbs. She gasped when Justin pushed in behind her, holding her breasts.

"Lick them," Justin urged, and Mitch did just that, placing his mouth over one distended nipple.

Her legs buckled, but Justin held onto her as she arched into Mitch's mouth, the sensation shooting straight to her pussy. She gripped Justin's forearms, crying out as Mitch sucked and licked her nipple—first one, then the other. Justin's cock was hard against her ass. She could only imagine the picture they presented. Her, naked from the waist up, leaning against one man while another sucked her nipples.

She wasn't unwrapping her Christmas gift. She *was* the gift, and she was the one being unwrapped. And she wouldn't have it any other way, especially when Mitch tugged on her dress, letting it drop to her ankles. He bent down and pulled the dress away from her feet, leaving her wearing only her red silk thong.

"Now there's one hell of a sweet Christmas present," Mitch said, his eyes sparkling with devilish delight. He stayed on his knees, pulled the fabric aside and planted his mouth over her throbbing sex.

Amy cried out. Mitch's tongue licked the length of her, lapping up the juices pouring from her pussy. Before she could recover, he moved to her clit, drawing slow, lazy circles around the tight bud until she wanted to scream.

"Is it everything you imagined?" Justin asked, his voice low and husky. He plucked her nipples as he watched Mitch over her shoulders.

"Yes," she managed through gritted teeth. "Oh, yes."

"It's only just beginning, babe. We're going to make you come over and over again."

She might not survive Christmas Eve. She didn't think she cared. Not when Mitch was bringing her closer and closer to orgasm, and Justin's fingers danced over her nipples, his tongue laving her neck until her pulse threatened to jump out her throat.

She was dizzy, overwhelmed, tuned into every sensation, trying to commit it all to memory, yet wanting to enjoy it as it happened. She was close, oh so close, and she began to pump against Mitch's face. He teased his fingers along her swollen slit, sliding two inside her pussy to pump fuck her in slow gentle rhythm as he latched onto her sex and began swirling his tongue around her clit.

"Oh, God. I'm coming," she cried, tensing against Justin as she flooded Mitch's face. Her climax was a whirling vortex, zapping her of thought and strength. Wave after wave crashed inside her like she was making her way onto the shore. She rode it with abandon, enjoying every single pulse until she went limp against Justin. He held onto her, tilting her head back to kiss her, forcing his tongue into her mouth and licking at hers until she was wound up and sparking with arousal yet again.

Mitch kissed his way up her belly, her ribs, lingering at her breasts to tease her nipples again. She didn't think she could cope with this much sensation, yet the more they gave her, the more she craved. Mitch pulled her from Justin's arms, gathering her close and kissing her deeply, letting her taste her come on his mouth. She licked at him, whimpering with need as he palmed her buttocks and drew her against his erection.

She heard the rustle of clothing behind her. She shivered, thinking about Justin getting naked.

"Can you stand, honey?" Mitch asked.

She nodded. "Barely."

Mitch grinned, placed her gently on her own two feet, then pulled his shirt off and began to unzip his pants. Amy swallowed. Justin tapped her shoulder and passed her a cocktail. She took a long swallow, parched from her whimpering and panting—God, she'd been like a bitch in heat, begging for it. And she wanted more. Her sexual drought was over. The monsoon had begun and she was eager to stand right in the middle of it and get soaked.

Especially when Mitch removed his pants. He was so different from Justin. Justin's chest was bare, Mitch had a crop of dark hair covering his chest. His cock was long where Justin's was thick. Her pussy quivered at the thought of what was going to happen, anticipation trickling down her thigh.

Amy wanted to experience both of them, inside her, to suck one while the other fucked her. She wanted it in so many ways, just like in her fantasies.

And she wanted it now.

She turned to Justin, threading her fingers through his hair as she pressed her lips to his, wanting to make sure he understood how much this meant to her. Was this easy for him, watching her with another man? Or did he even care? She didn't quite know where the two of them stood, relationship wise. Or if what they had could even be considered a relationship. She pushed those worries to the back of her mind for now. The only thing she concentrated on was the feel of his lips sliding across hers—so smooth, yet so demanding. The way he crushed her body to his in such a possessive manner thrilled her. He made her feel like she was the only woman for him.

Maybe she was.

Maybe she wanted to be.

Don't think, Amy. Not now. Just feel.

As she kissed Justin, Mitch moved behind her, his cock rubbing against her hip as he leaned in to press his lips against the column of her spine. He drew her away from Justin's greedy mouth, dragging her onto his lap on the sofa.

"Condoms are in the downstairs bathroom, left hand drawer," Mitch said.

Justin nodded and left the room. Mitch drew Amy's hair to the side and licked her neck.

"God you smell good. I could lick you all over."

She shuddered at the wet warmth of Mitch's tongue against her skin, his hands roaming her body and his cock pressing against her lower back.

"I need to fuck you, Amy. I need to fuck you while Justin watches. Do you want that?"

Mitch painted an erotic visual she couldn't wait to explore. "Yes. I want that, Mitch." She was so wet she was drowning in it, throbbing incessantly at the thought of what was about to happen.

Justin returned, his gaze riveted on Mitch's wandering hands. Amy's legs were spread over Mitch's thighs, exposing her pussy to both of them.

"Damn, you have a pretty pussy, Amy," Justin said, taking his cock in his hand and stroking it as he stood beside the edge of the sofa.

Mitch cupped Amy's thighs and pulled her up so her butt rested on his stomach. "I don't want to wait," he said, holding out his hand to Justin. Justin grabbed a condom packet and handed it to Mitch. Once Mitch had it on, he positioned Amy over his cock, letting her slide down onto the head.

In the meantime, Justin leaned over, dragging his fingers through her hair to grab her attention. He wanted her mouth, kissing her again just as Mitch seated his cock fully inside her. Amy pulsed around him, overwhelmed with sensation. Mitch's shaft moved in and out of her with a slow, deliberate rhythm, his hands covering her breasts and doing delicious things to her nipples. Justin licked at her tongue, then pulled away and held her head in place as he replaced his mouth with his cock. She grabbed his cockhead between her lips, licking the wide crest before capturing it in her mouth and sucking it with a greedy hunger.

She had them both now, and Mitch held onto her hips, fucking her with gentle ease while Justin stroked his cock between her lips—soft velvet combing her tongue with salty liquid, signaling his pleasure. She stared up into his tightly strained face. He was watching her, his gaze switching between her face and where she and Mitch were connected. He held the back of her head as he pumped into her mouth, and she reached up to cradle his balls in her hand, giving them a tender squeeze. He hissed and tightened his fist in her hair. She knew he held back, trying not to bruise her throat by fucking her mouth hard, but she wanted his passion, especially with Mitch being so soft and gentle with his stroking of her pussy.

She needed more, and let Mitch know. It was time to direct this game. She leaned back and took Justin's cock out of her mouth, then maneuvered herself into a standing position.

"Need a break?" Mitch asked.

She shook her head. "Oh no. Just a position change. I want you to lean back on the sofa this way." She directed Mitch to recline against one end of the couch. When he did, she straddled him, sliding down on his cock until he was buried deep inside her. She pulsed, gripping him, and Mitch held onto her hips, pumping upward. She gasped, fighting for control, then gave Justin a look over her shoulder.

"Are you sure?" he asked, coming toward her, his cock still wet from her mouth.

"Yes. And hurry." She was already anticipating the moment he would fill her—they would fill her. Just like her fantasies.

She turned away and placed her palms on Mitch's chest. He smiled up at her, swept her hair away from her face, and lifted his hips, driving his shaft deeper. She gasped, her lips parted, sucking in air.

Justin kneeled on the sofa, his hands on her buttocks.

"Tell me again this is what you want, Amy."

She reached behind her, her fingers curling over his cock. "Justin, please. Yes, I want you."

"Christ," he whispered, right before he spread her ass cheeks and cool liquid spread over her anus, followed by his fingers, coating her with lube.

Amy turned away, tangling her fingers in the crisp mat of hair on Mitch's chest, her pussy contracting around his cock. She heard the foil packet tearing, then felt Justin maneuvering behind her.

"Have you ever been fucked in the ass, Amy?" Justin asked, caressing her lower back.

"No."

"Ever stuck a toy in there, like a dildo?"

God, did he know all her secrets? "Yes."

"Did you fantasize about two men fucking you?" Mitch's gaze was intent, curious, his eyes like the crystal water they'd sailed over earlier today.

"All the time, Mitch." She dug her fingers into his chest as Justin fit the head of his cock against her anus.

"Hang on, babe. Relax and breathe through this. If it hurts, tell me and I'll stop."

Mitch halted his movements and Justin took it slow, penetrating her with just the head of his cock. It burned, but she'd expected it. She wasn't lying when she said she'd fucked herself in the ass before. She'd double penetrated herself with her toys, always imagining what it would be like to be fucked by two men simultaneously.

Now it was really happening. She wasn't going to stop.

Instead, she relaxed her muscles and breathed deeply, leaning forward against Mitch's chest, lifting her ass in the air. And then Justin pushed in deeper, sliding more of his cock past her tight muscles. She blew in, out, feeling every inch of him penetrate her until he was fully sheathed in her ass.

She stilled, her eyes closed as she captured the moment, adjusted, really felt them. Both of them were inside her, barely separated, no doubt able to feel each other. She'd never felt more filled, could hardly breathe through the sensations pummeling her from both sides. Her clit was nestled against Mitch's pelvis, and the slightest movement set off a storm of vibration. Her pussy quivered, her anus tightened, and then Mitch and Justin began to move.

Like pistons, Mitch drove up while Justin pulled back, then vice versa, and the feeling was incredible, like a slow, drugging assault, ripping her apart in slow motion. They didn't hurry, didn't ravage her with hard strokes. Instead, they took their time and treated her with gentle care.

She had always thought this would be wild and crazy, that it would hurt, that she would be torn apart by insane, crazy sex. Instead, it was terribly emotional, and she was coming undone because of it. Justin spread his body over her back, kissing her neck, whispering to her as he speared her with his cock, and Mitch held onto her hands, encouraging her to let go.

How could she not with these two at the helm? She gave herself up to the sensations and moved with them, holding onto Mitch's hands, tossing her head back against Justin, and reveled in being sandwiched between them as they took her to the edge, then over.

When she came, it was like being squeezed into the most exquisite death imaginable. Her pussy gripped Mitch's cock as she spiraled out of control, and the muscles of her anus gripped

Justin's shaft. She felt the contractions everywhere and it intensified her orgasm tenfold. Fighting for air, she tilted her head back and could only let out a croaking sound and violently shudder while they both held onto her, rocketing into their own orgasms. This time they did pound into her, Mitch driving deep and Justin pumping hard into her ass.

Spent, she fell forward, Justin wrapping his arm around her waist and holding tight to her, his heart pounding a fast rhythm against her back.

It took her a long while to recover. By the time she could move, Justin had already withdrawn and left the room. Mitch leaned up, picking her up with him and carrying her to the bathroom.

Justin already had the shower on and was waiting for them. Mitch handed her over with a soft kiss and a whispered 'thank you', and Justin pulled her into Mitch's oversized shower, letting the warm spray soothe her overused body.

He kissed her, a gentle brush of his lips across hers, then he washed her all over before taking care of himself.

"You okay?" he asked after he was rinsed.

She nodded, because she was without words, could only smile and remember.

It had been everything she could have ever wanted, and she couldn't think of two other men who could have made it better for her.

Justin dried her off. Their clothes were lying in the dressing area outside the bathroom, and they got dressed. Mitch was already showered and waiting for them in the living room when they came out.

Mitch pulled Amy into his arms and kissed her, a soft, lingering kiss that curled her toes. He dragged his thumb across her bottom lip and she shuddered.

"No regrets?" he asked.

She shook her head and gave Mitch a warm smile. "None at all."

Mitch nodded. "I'm flying out first thing tomorrow. I have to be in Australia the day after Christmas and the whole time zone change whacks me out, so this is goodbye for us until the next time I see you."

Amy gripped Mitch's forearms. "I don't know what to say other than thank you for giving me such an incredible gift."

Mitch grinned. "Believe me, sweetheart. It was my pleasure." He pulled her into his arms for a hug, then released her and bear hugged Justin.

"Anytime you want to leave that stuffy firm, I've got a job for you," Mitch said.

"I'll think about it," Justin said with a wink. "You take care of yourself, old man."

Mitch snorted. "Merry Christmas, Amy."

"Same to you, Mitch."

She and Justin left, walking hand in hand back to their bungalows. But instead of seeing her to her room, Justin took her to his, pulling back the covers on his bed and unzipping her dress.

"Tonight I want you to sleep with me," he said.

Amy had no objection, just let her dress fall to the ground. She crawled into his bed and let him curl up behind her and pull her close.

This was perfect. Almost too perfect. Because it wasn't real.

It had all been one fantastic fantasy.

And with tomorrow, came reality. She already knew the reality. Was intimately familiar with the way things really were, the way they were going to be after this idyllic few days in

Hawaii.

Nothing was going to change.

But tonight, she was nestled in Justin's arms and had just experienced the fantasy of a lifetime.

She'd worry about the reality later.

"Do you want to talk about this?" Justin asked, his warm breath tickling the hair on the back of her neck.

"No. I don't ever want to talk about it again." Though she'd relive it, over and over again. Not just the ménage with Justin and Mitch, but every moment she'd spent with Justin.

"Sure. Whatever you want."

She waited, but in a few moments his breathing evened out and she was certain he'd fallen asleep.

Amy exhaled, ran her fingers over Justin's hand. Touching him made her belly quiver.

That was so not good. Being here with Justin in Hawaii, spending time with him, talking with him, made her realize the truth.

She was in love with him.

Even having sex with another man hadn't changed that. It had only reaffirmed her feelings for Justin.

Mitch was hot. Sexy. Rich. Successful. Older than her, and a prime catch for someone in Amy's position.

Fucking Mitch hadn't made a damn difference.

She wanted Justin. And only him.

And she wasn't going to have him. Their relationship was doomed from the start and she was putting a stop to it first thing tomorrow. Cutting it off now, before either of them started hurting more, would be for the best.

She blinked back tears, hating that she'd allowed it to get

this far.

She already missed him. This was going to be so damn difficult, but they'd weather through it. She knew Justin would see the reason behind her decision. His career was as important as hers. He'd understand. This had been just a fling for both of them. Fun, but that's all it was and all it could ever be.

People like them didn't fall in love, didn't have relationships.

They had careers. And that's all they had.

It was time to get back to her career. Fun time was over.

Chapter Eight

Justin had woke Christmas morning alone. He'd like to say he was shocked to find Amy gone, but he wasn't.

He'd expected it. He'd also expected to find that she'd checked out, taken an early morning flight back to Los Angeles, hadn't left a note.

It had been one hell of a Christmas Day.

Amy had run like hell after their night with Mitch. Just as he expected her to.

Justin took it as a really good sign.

He was really shocked when he got back to work the day after Christmas to find Amy had switched some cases they were working on together, assigning them to another attorney. His assistant said Amy claimed she was overloaded and just making some adjustments. When Justin went to confront Amy, her secretary said Amy had taken a few days off.

Amy's assistant seemed as surprised as Justin, since Amy never took time off. Her secretary said she'd be out of the office and working at home until after the new year.

Justin holed up in his office and pondered this new development.

It was even better than he'd thought. She was cutting all ties with him, and it sure as hell wasn't because she hated him.

Miss Amy Parker, Esquire, was in love with him, and this was her way of dealing with it.

But now it was time for Justin to play his hand.

He had some serious decisions to make. And a phone call.

Then he had to go see Amy.

Amy grabbed the steaming cup of tea and padded into her living room, sliding onto her sofa and glaring at the laptop screen.

Adjusting her client files and trading off with one of the other attorneys meant getting up to speed on new cases. More work.

And her powers of concentration were shot. She hadn't slept since she'd been back from Hawaii.

She missed Justin. A stab of guilt pained her stomach, but she pushed it aside.

He hadn't called her. Had she really expected him to since she left his bed in the early hours Christmas morning, left no note, and then obviously told him what she thought of him by cutting all professional ties? Not only wouldn't they be sleeping together anymore, they'd barely be working together.

She really was an ice queen, wasn't she? She'd become quite adept at burying her emotions so the only thing anyone saw was a cool professional exterior. Icy. Unapproachable.

Too bad it wasn't working on herself. She was miserable, couldn't eat, couldn't sleep and she goddamn hurt inside.

This was for the best? For whose best? Hers? Justin's?

It sucked.

The doorbell rang. She sighed, setting the tea down and heading to the door. It was probably the messenger from work delivering the case files she'd asked for. She opened the door, shocked to find Justin standing there.

"Justin."

"Amy."

Before she could utter a word, he'd brushed past her and entered her apartment.

"Uh, come in why don't you?"

He had a package in his hand. A Christmas present. A big box tied with an oversized red bow.

"Thanks. I think I will." He turned to her, surveying her apartment. "What? No Christmas tree?"

She rolled her eyes. "I'm never here. A tree seemed pointless."

"How appropriately humbug of you. I'll just set this down here, then." He laid it on her coffee table.

"Justin, really, you shouldn't have."

"Yes, I know. You don't deserve it. I did it anyway."

She crossed her arms, feeling profoundly uncomfortable. "Why are you here?"

He took a seat on her sofa, grimacing at the laptop. "Obviously you're not at home because you're sick. Your cheeks are pink and you look fine to me. My guess is you're avoiding me."

"I am not. I just needed to catch up on some work and wanted to do it uninterrupted."

"Oh, yeah. Learning all those new cases because you swapped client files with Jamison."

She sank onto the other end of the sofa, hating the confrontation that was coming, but knowing it was inevitable. "Justin. Let's be realistic."

"Okay. Go ahead." He shrugged out of his jacket and slung

it over the back of the sofa.

Amy wanted to run her hands over his cashmere sweater. Or under his cashmere sweater to feel his smooth, heated skin and the play of muscles in his abdomen. Instead, she steeled herself, reminding herself why she'd done this in the first place.

"We have no future together."

"Really? Why?"

"You're younger than me."

"Do you really consider that a valid excuse?"

No. "When I'm fifty you'd be—"

"Forty-five. I can do math, Amy. I still don't get your point. I don't love you because of your age. And I think it's damn hot that you're older than me."

Oh, shit. "You love me?"

"You graduated summa cum laude from Stanford. If you can't figure out that I love you, then I'm really disappointed in your perceptive powers. Of course I love you. Would I put up with your bullshit if I didn't?"

Her throat constricted and she fought back tears. "Love doesn't last."

"And you base this on?"

"May/December romances never do. I'll get wrinkly. I'll get jowls."

His lips lifted. "I'll put a bag over your head when I fuck you."

She couldn't help it. She snorted. "That wasn't funny."

"And I don't love you because of how you look. I love you because of who you are. You're brilliant. You can be funny. You love adventure and you have no fear. We have the same backgrounds. We're both driven and competitive and I like being with you. I like making love to you, like having you sleeping next to me at night. Do you think five years make any difference to me?"

No, she didn't. Dammit, she didn't. Her mind whirled trying to come up with something else.

"We're constantly competing with each other in the firm. It would destroy us."

He grabbed the box and placed it in her lap. "Open your Christmas present, Amy."

"I—"

"Just open the goddamn box."

"Fine." Anything to get through this and get him out of her apartment before she fell apart. She pulled the bow on the giant box and lifted the lid, lifting out miles and miles of tissue paper. At the bottom of the box was an envelope. She pulled the envelope out and slanted a quizzical look at Justin.

He nodded. "Open it."

She sliced through the envelope and opened the single paper in there. Her blood went cold when she read the contents.

"You didn't," she whispered, her gaze shooting to Justin.

"I did. This afternoon."

"Oh, Justin. Why?"

"I turned in my resignation at McKenzie and Shoals for two reasons. First, because I love you and I don't want this whole thing about us being competitive and you thinking I wanted to fuck my way to the top—or using you and our relationship— coming between us. Now it's not between us anymore."

She couldn't believe he'd resigned. He'd been working his way through that firm for years. He was poised on the brink of partnership. "Are you insane?"

He moved closer to her, tossed the box and all the paper on

the floor and took Amy's hand in his. "No, Amy. I'm in love."

Shock froze her in place, her mind refusing to register what he'd done on her behalf. Because he loved her? "You've ruined your career."

"No. I've just started it."

"What do you mean?"

"What do you think of Garrett and Parker?"

Her pulse raced. "Garrett and Parker?"

He smiled. "Yeah. You, me, our own law firm?"

"You've lost your mind." Excitement warred with trepidation. "We don't have the capital for that kind of venture. Or the clients."

Justin arched a brow. "No, that's true. *We* don't have the capital to start our own firm."

It hit her instantly. "Mitch."

"Yes."

"Oh my God. Mitch would do that?"

"Of course he would. And he'll move all his business to us, too."

Amy couldn't breathe. "Why, Justin?"

"Because I love you, and because neither one of us is making partner fast enough at McKenzie and Shoals. You know it and I know it. They're a great firm, but they're slow to promote. And you and I are ambitious go getters who want to push the envelope. They're not right for us, Amy. We need our own gig."

He was right. Dear God, he was right. He'd seen it where she hadn't. All this time, she'd been playing it safe, toeing the line, doing everything right in the hopes to make it to the top. And trying to keep her peers from getting there before her—like

Justin.

Justin had taken the risk and was offering her the opportunity of a lifetime, and his love, too.

"All you have to do is say yes, Amy."

He'd done all this because he loved her. And she hadn't even told him—

"I love you, Justin. Before we go any further, you need to know that."

"I know you do."

"You do?"

He grinned. "When I woke up Christmas morning and you weren't in my bed or even in Hawaii anymore, I knew it."

"How?"

"You ran because you were scared of your feelings. If you didn't care, you'd have gotten on that plane back to L.A. with me and wouldn't have blinked."

She tried to take it all in. "Sometimes you scare me because you know me so well."

"That's why we'll make such good partners. Nobody understands me like you do. Nobody is less willing to put up with my bullshit as you are."

She laughed. "We make quite a pair, don't we?"

"There's something else."

"Okay."

"I read the email you sent to your friend Gloria. The one where you said you wanted a ménage."

Her eyes widened. "What? When?"

"A week or so before we left for Hawaii. You'd tossed your laptop at me to pull a document off, and I couldn't find it so I thought it was in your email attachments. I found it there." He at least had the decency to look guilty.

"That's how you knew about my fantasy."

"Yeah."

"I should be furious with you for invading my privacy."

"Yes, you should."

But she wasn't. He'd given her the greatest gift she could have ever asked for.

"And another thing, Amy."

"What is it?"

"That night with Mitch was great. It was hot. You were incredible. But it's never going to happen again."

"It isn't?"

"No. I don't share what's mine. You had your one and only ménage."

She let her eyes drift closed, unable to believe she'd found a man like Justin. Then she opened them and saw him—really saw him, for the brilliant, loving man he was. He'd done all that for her, to make her happy.

"I really do love you," she said, palming his cheeks and brushing her lips across his. He pulled her closer, deepening the kiss, sliding his tongue inside her mouth to claim her with passionate intent.

Desire flared and burst inside her. Going two days without Justin had been horrible. She'd felt empty inside. Now she needed him to fill her.

His mouth still doing delicious things to hers, he dragged her flat onto the sofa, searching under her T-shirt and finding her breasts, skimming her nipples until she writhed with need. But when she tried to lift up so she could undress her, he held her down.

"Stay there," he said, reaching for her sweatpants and jerking them off, leaving her naked from the waist down. He slid off the couch, using his hip to push the coffee table out of the way. He dug a condom out of his pocket and unzipped his jeans, shoving them down his thighs.

"Hurry," she whispered, lifting her hips while he applied the condom. He pulled her to the end of the sofa and plunged inside her so hard she cried out, her body flexing to accommodate him. He held onto her while he pumped her with relentless strokes, claiming her, possessing her in a way only Justin could. She raked his forearms with her nails, her need for him almost violent in its intensity.

She couldn't get enough, pushing her pussy onto his cock, wanting him deeper, needing him to fuck her harder. Her pussy poured over him, over them both. She was so close and she wanted him to finish with her.

"Come with me," she said, grinding her sex against him as she tried to hold back. But she was tightening, spiraling, losing control.

Justin growled, shuddered against her and she climaxed, spasming around his hot cock, bucking up off the couch as she gave him all she had.

He lay his head on her breasts as they recovered and she stroked his hair, unable to believe this magnificent man was all hers. A man she'd stupidly tried to throw away.

Relaxed, feeling Justin in her arms and knowing he was never going to leave, she whispered, "Parker and Garrett."

Justin lifted his head. "Huh?"

"Parker and Garrett. I think that sounds better."

"In your dreams. We're going alphabetical. Garrett and Parker."

"We're going by age. Parker and Garrett."

"You won't win. I have the bigger dick."

She gave him a knowing smile. "But I have the pussy."

He thrust against her, his cock swelling within her again. "I can tell these negotiations might go well into the night."

She sighed and gave him a wicked smile. "I'm used to working all night."

About the Author

To learn more about Jaci Burton, please visit www.jaciburton.com. Send an email to Jaci Burton at jaci@jaciburton.com or join her Yahoo! group at http://groups.yahoo.com/group/writeminded_readers/ to join in the fun with other readers as well as her newsletter at www.jaciburton.com/news.html for updates about future releases.

Look for these titles by
Jaci Burton

Now Available:

Rescue Me
Nothing Personal
Show Me
Dare To Love

Coming Soon:

Sneak Peek (print anthology with Shelley Bradley)
Unraveled
Crimson Ties

To Do List

Lauren Dane

Dedication

This one is for my grandma Minnie who taught me that anything is possible when you work hard to achieve your dreams. I miss you and your sopas but you're my heart forever.

Thanks to Angie for her editing and for not ignoring me when I IM her with stupid questions.

As always, thanks go to my friends and family who show me unfailing support in this journey, even when it makes me grumpy, sleep deprived and I raid their lives to put in my books. Ray, thank you for being the kind of man who knew I'd love the pair of Chucks with the black sheep on the heel.

Chapter One

Belle shivered as Rafe's mouth touched her neck. A sense of total and utter unreality stole over her. Here she stood, in the dark, wrapped around the guy she'd had a major crush on since she'd been twelve years old. Hell, that very morning, she never even imagined he'd thought of her this way.

"You taste good, Belle. Delicious and sweet with just a little spice." The low vibration of his voice echoed up her spine. The warmth of his hands at her hips, just barely touching the bare skin peeking below the hem of her sweater and above the waist of her trousers, sent waves of pleasure through her.

Even as she searched for words, his tongue made its way, slow and sinuous, up her neck and to her ear. His breath stirred tendrils of hair that'd escaped the barrette holding it back from her face.

"I think I'm going to need to kiss you, now. I've been wondering all night long if that lip gloss is flavored. Are you old school like that?"

Holy sweet baby Jesus on a skateboard. How on earth was she supposed to answer him when he said stuff like that? When he pressed against her, his body work-hard and strong. His cock a solid, hot weight against her belly.

"Watermelon," she managed to gasp.

"Well now, I definitely need a taste of that."

He angled his head and his mouth moved to hers, his clear, sleepy brown eyes seeing right straight through her.

And when he kissed her, her entire body went boneless as she held on, her fingers digging into the material of his coat. His mouth was softer than she'd imagined, hot, wet, he tasted of coffee, salt and something else she couldn't identify but wouldn't ever forget.

His kiss was slow and heady. He took his time like a man who knew what he was about. Like a man who knew she wasn't going to bolt. He explored her mouth, his teeth catching her bottom lip, his hands firming their hold, settling beneath the sweater, fingers splayed against the sensitive, bare skin of her hips. His thumbs slid slowly back and forth, back and forth in the hollow of her hip bones.

Her nipples throbbed in time with the slide of his thumbs, shooting straight to her clit.

"Belle? Rafe? You guys there?" Brian called from the other room and Rafe stood back, breaking the kiss. At least his chest heaved and he appeared to be as affected by the kiss as she had been. Cripes, she wasn't sure when the last time a kiss had nearly made her come, or even if a kiss had ever so aroused her.

"Yeah. I'm just helping Belle bring her suitcases in," Rafe answered Belle's oldest brother without moving. He grinned at her slowly and dragged his gaze up above her head. She followed and noted the mistletoe.

"Oh!" She blushed, mortified. Here she'd thought he was on fire for her and it was just the damned mistletoe? "Duh."

He reached and took her chin in his fingers, shaking his head. "No, Belle. I've wanted to kiss you for a very long time, the mistletoe just gave me an excuse. But now that I've felt your nipples as you kissed me, now that I know your taste? I'm going to kiss you as often as I can."

"Oh," she sighed again. Yeah, it was totally obvious she was a powerful attorney who made her living with her ability to speak coherently.

He chuckled and grabbed her suitcases. "I'm going to put these in the guest room and then we can get on over to your parents' for dinner."

Belle heaved a sigh as she leaned against the wall to keep from melting into a puddle of goo. Raphael Bettencourt had just laid the hottest kiss of her entire life on her. *Rafe.* The object of many a fantasy and he'd...his mouth...it was...oh wow!

"Belle? You okay? I know you're tired. Mom and Dad would understand if you'd rather call it a night." Brian came into the front hall, looking at her worry clear on his face.

She'd been late getting out of San Francisco, heading home for a few days to spend Christmas with her family when she'd had a blow out just miles outside of Davis. Thank goodness Brian and Rafe had come to help.

"You guys didn't have to come out, you know. I told you I'd have called Triple A." She stood straight, enjoying the warm feeling she still had in her stomach.

"Shut up. Your tire is changed and tomorrow we'll get you out to replace the old one. You don't need Triple A, you have family. Now, are you okay? You look really pale and you've lost at least fifteen pounds since the last time I saw you. That was a year ago though." He glared at her.

She smoothed down the front of her clothing and tucked her hair back. "Brian, no one knows how busted I look more than I do, okay?" She was so tired. She'd been working eighty-hour weeks for the last year, most notably the last seven months on one all-encompassing project. But it was over and she was taking the first actual time off since December of the year before. Christ, twelve months of eighty-hour weeks and not a single day off. She hadn't been outside in the daylight except to walk into the courthouse so of course she was pale.

"You don't look busted. You're beautiful and you know it. Damn it, Belle, you work too hard! No job is worth this insanity. Your health is important, more important than a corner office. How long has it been since you've had any time off?" Brian searched her face.

"Look, Doctor Taylor, I know, okay? Do you think I want to spend every freaking moment of my life working?" Before she could truly get upset, Rafe came back toward the front hall and she stopped herself.

"I'm not going to let this slide, Belle. You can't do this to yourself and you know Mom and Dad are going to say the same thing when they see you." Brian put an arm around her shoulder and nodded at Rafe.

"Give it a rest, Brian. She's here isn't she? I'll put her to work, get her out in the fresh air and sunlight and your mom will fatten her up." Rafe kissed her cheek and opened the front door. "Now, let's go on over to dinner before your dad sends a search party out."

"Wait! Let me change clothes. I came straight from work." Belle disentangled herself from her brother.

"You know where the guest room is." Rafe winked.

Good God, she'd be just next door to his room, connected by an adjoining bath. She'd been the one who'd told her brother what a great idea it would be to take over the large west wing of Rafe's ginormous house while Brian waited for his own place to be remodeled.

She pulled a red sweater from her suitcase, carefully hanging up the business black cashmere, and exchanged the gray wool trousers for soft denim jeans and boots. Her hair fell from the heavy knot at the base of her neck and she shook it out.

With a smile, she re-applied the watermelon lip gloss and headed out to meet her brother and Rafe.

"Much better. You still look too thin but boots and jeans are much nicer than those stuffy business clothes you had on." Brian held his hand out and she took it.

"Be quiet. Belle looked lovely in her other outfit."

The two friends bickered and laughed, filling Belle in on all the gossip as they headed over to Belle and Brian's parents' house just ten minutes away.

When Brian pulled down the long gravel drive leading to the main house on the organic farm her father and brothers worked, she rolled the windows down.

Cold air rushed in with the scent of wet grass. Of hay and the river in the far distance. The house was ablaze with light and the sight of it brought tears to her eyes. Her father had hung the Christmas lights along the roof of the house. No plain white lights for her dad, no way. He favored the colorful lights with the big bulbs. The large elms and a few fruit and almond trees in the spacious front and side yard were festooned with lights as well and she saw the big tree through the living room window. It would still be bare, they'd decorate it over the next two nights as a family. Same as they'd done every year of her life.

Her parents would have a full house with grandparents, assorted children, spouses, and grandchildren running around. Within the next few days, her cousins, aunts and uncles would also arrive. Which is why she was staying at Brian and Rafe's— and her lips thought that was a fine idea.

When they got out, Loopy, one of their labs, ran toward her

with a goofy grin, his tongue hanging out. She paused to bend and kiss the top of his head and scratch behind an ear.

"He's getting gray. Got a bit of arthritis the vet said." Brian ran a hand over the dog's back.

"He still gets on the tractor and goes out with me several times a week. Loopy has plenty of get up and go." Rafe tucked the hair behind Belle's ear absently. When he headed toward the house, she watched him from behind and took her time catching up.

Belle had always loved Rafe as one of their extended family. He was a good man, funny and flirtatious. He loved farming and their community and had dedicated himself to helping her dad get their organic operation started four years before and also helped run the Bettencourt family dairy.

Life was slower here in Davis. Harder in a lot of ways. Her dad was up before dawn most days and there were times when she was growing up when things were very tight. But there was money for college and they'd always had enough for the truly important stuff. They ate, they had clothes on their back and they never wanted for attention or love.

"Belle? Sweetie pie, is that you?" her mother called out from the porch and Belle bounded past her brother and Rafe and into her mom's arms.

Belle breathed in a bit of White Shoulders along with pot roast and if she wasn't wrong, apple pie. Rock on.

"I'm sorry I'm late."

"You can't help a blow out. Thank goodness you weren't hurt. Now, you're here and that's what matters." Her mother pulled back and gave Belle a very critical once over and frowned. "Good gracious, girl! Look at you. I don't like it one bit. You're too thin and you have dark circles under your eyes. I made those eyes, Annabelle, I don't like you mistreating yourself." Her mother raised one eyebrow in her direction as she towed Belle into the house where it seemed like half the known universe shouted out hellos.

"Thank God we can finally eat!" her youngest brother Kevin bellowed.

"I'm only forty-five minutes late. I left San Francisco at five after six so that's darned good time with all the traffic mess and then the blow out. I told Dad to have everyone start without me."

She said all this as she accepted hugs and kisses from the family, including her very pregnant sister.

"As if Mom is going to let us touch the roast when you're not here. You look tired, even if it's damned good to see you. Skinny and pale. I don't like the dark circles under your eyes. You getting any sleep? Don't you eat anything more than wheat grass and coffee?" Chelsea, her older sister and the only other female Taylor child, murmured into her ear as she hugged her.

"Yes, I know. You're the tenth person to tell me that. It's such an ego boost to come home. How are you?" Belle ran a hand over her sister's belly.

"Pregnant. Don't tell these clowns but Mom let me have a sandwich already. Sit before Kevin or Scott busts a gut moaning about how hungry they are. Grandma hasn't complained. If an eighty-five-year-old woman can live without eating, you know they can."

"I can hear you, Chelsea," Scott, her next older brother called out from across the table where he helped their grandmother into a chair.

"Duh." Chelsea laughed and let her husband Bill lower her into a chair.

"Come sit next to me, Belle."

She looked up to see Rafe pulling a chair out for her. Damn he looked good. Big brown eyes, dark hair always in dire need of a trim, Raphael Bettencourt was big and muscled and worked hard out in the sun all day long. He was good-looking farm boy personified and he and Brian had been best friends since the second grade when the Bettencourts moved to Davis and started their family-run dairy. And he'd totally made love to her mouth not even twenty minutes before. Yeah, vacation was already better than working.

He kissed her cheek as she sat at the table and she tried not to make a big deal out of sniffing him. It'd be nice if he'd take one for the team, or twelve, to help her relax. She smiled to herself as warm, hard male surrounded her when he bent around to help her get the chair in.

"Thanks, Rafe. I like that sweater. Did one of your smitten harem make it for you?"

He laughed and the sound shot to all sorts of low places. "Now, Annabelle, jealousy doesn't become you. I'd be perfectly happy to add you to my harem any old time."

Brian smacked the top of Rafe's head before shoving a bowl of peas into his hands. "Stop coming on to my sister. Make yourself useful."

"What kept you so late anyway? I thought you said you were only working half a day today?" Kevin called across the table as the noise rose.

"That was the plan. I got into work before six this morning. But you know what they say about the best laid plans. Anyway, I'm trying to rush out the door and some senior partner wants me to stay back and finish up." Belle didn't elaborate, it wasn't necessary anyway. He'd berated her for taking vacation when she led by nearly a third above the highest billable hours of anyone else in the firm. Jerk.

"Who are these people to think they own every bit of your time? It's been a year, Annabelle. You are a member of this family and it's high time you remembered that," her grandmother admonished from a few seats down.

"Nana, I know. I haven't forgotten I'm a member of the family. It's hard trying to make it into that corner office. It takes time. This case I just finished up is really important and I think it will make me. I'm here though and I will be for the next five days. I turned off my cell phone and left my laptop at home. It's all family all the time. I promise." Belle nearly laughed at the look on her grandmother's face as she waved a hand.

"These people! No values. Working you younger attorneys like slaves. I bet *they* all go on vacation." Her father harrumphed and Kevin winked at Belle from his place across the table.

"Dad, Nana, Belle has worked hard. It takes a lot of hours to get as far as she has. She went to law school and we all knew she'd be busy when she started at the firm. I don't think it's fair to say she's forgotten her family because she's doing what all young lawyers at big firms have to, to get ahead. No one complained when I was in residency." Brian, her defender, squeezed her hand under the table.

"Of course not. I know Nana didn't mean it like that." Her mother frowned. "But it's been a year since we've had all our children at this table. We miss Belle. We are proud of you, honey."

"Of her accomplishments, always. Not of the way she looks. Too thin. Pale like she hasn't seen the sun in a very long time. And if you take what I said personally, I'd have to spank you." Her grandmother sipped her water calmly and Belle gave in to the smile threatening her face. "And you, Brian, you had residency and then set up practice here in town. We didn't see you often for about two years and then it all calmed down. We want Belle to be successful but that doesn't mean we want to trade her away and never see her again."

Belle knew it. She knew her life had spun out of control and she'd had no time at all for anything but working. It was a crappy existence and she'd told herself as she'd driven away from the city that evening that some to do lists and perhaps even a spreadsheet was in order. Her life wasn't the way she'd envisioned it, not at all.

Chapter Two

Rafe couldn't quite believe he'd actually kissed Belle in his front entry. But she'd been standing there, looking so damned delicious and remote in her business attire and the mistletoe had been so convenient, he'd had to give in.

And now that he'd tasted her? He planned to do it a lot more before she disappeared back to San Francisco for another year.

Yes, she was pale and too thin as people had pointed out, but her pretty blue eyes had glittered in the lights hung in the entry and even now, the candles on the table gave her skin a warm glow. His fingers itched to slide through that gorgeous spill of dark blonde hair hanging in shiny waves to her waist.

Rafe had always thought of Annabelle Taylor as an obsessive, anal retentive, control freak of a little sister until five years prior at her law school graduation party. He wasn't sure what exact moment had brought about the change but suddenly, he'd looked and the girl he'd grown up helping his friend torment had transformed into a beautiful woman. Still a complete control freak, but he'd wanted to strip her naked and make her lose control ever since that day.

She'd worked so hard and he'd spent so much time organizing his family dairy and taking on the marketing and PR for the Taylors' organic farming venture that they'd never had the time.

From the look on her face and the tired way she held her shoulders, she needed some diversion in a major way and he was damned sure she wasn't getting any between the sheets.

Fate put her right next door to his bedroom and he wasn't one to look askance at fate now was he? When Belle went back to work after Christmas, she'd have some meat on her bones and a very satisfied glow about her.

"Here, have some pie." He put a giant slice of apple pie on her plate and she goggled at him. He knew it would rile her and get her mother's attention too. Rafe wasn't above using others to get what he needed done, done.

"Whoa there! I can't eat all that."

"You will eat every bit, Annabelle Louise!" her mother chided from her place just down the table. "Rafe, put some whipped cream on top and I'm sending down the ice cream too. It's fresh, Belle. I made it earlier today."

Rafe wisely held back a laugh when Belle sat back and didn't argue with her mother. The woman was raised right, didn't argue with her elders, so he knew when Rita Taylor backed him up on the pie, Belle would eat it.

"You involved her on purpose," Belle hissed without looking directly at him. She forked up a heaping mouthful and his cock threatened to burst from his jeans at the sound she made.

"I did. And I'd do it again to make you moan like that. Better yet, I have other ways to make you moan," he whispered in her ear.

"You think you're gonna shock me? Don't tease me, Rafe, because I'll totally take you up on your challenge," she said back in an undertone.

"Not a tease at all. Now eat your pie and ice cream." He

plopped a huge spoonful of freshly made vanilla on top of the pie. "You'll need your strength."

"You're going to have to roll me out of here." Belle patted her belly and groaned she was so full.

"Whatever it takes." Her mother handed her a sheet of paper. "It's the schedule. I expect to see you over here tomorrow by nine. We're going shopping and then we'll do lunch and wrapping. The next day we'll have tree trimming and after dinner tomorrow we'll do cranberry and popcorn garlands. The rest is on there. Your aunt and uncle will bring their RV and stay Christmas Eve and your cousins will all come in between now and then as well." Her mother kissed her cheek. "You all right staying over at Brian and Rafe's?"

"Of course! I know Nana and Poppa need a bedroom without stairs and you need to have Chelsea and the kids all in one place. It's just up the road and it'll be a heck of a lot quieter tomorrow morning than it'll be here."

"Gives me a reason not to be so sad my nest is empty after a week with the grandkids." Her mother winked. "We're doing lunch and you're going to talk to us about your job, so don't even try to avoid it."

"Good night, Mom." She hugged her mom and moved to her father. "And you too, Dad. I'll see you guys tomorrow."

Back at the house, Belle waved off Brian's attempt to get her to talk and headed straight for the guest room.

"She's going to work herself to death," Brian muttered to Rafe.

"I don't like it any more than you do. But you have to let her deal with it in her own way. Clearly she knows she has some prioritizing to do. If you push her too far, she'll pull away entirely."

"Shit. You have a thing for her don't you?" Brian leaned against the kitchen counter and watched Rafe.

"What makes you say that?"

"First of all, you didn't deny it right now, which you would have if I'd made the same comment about Chelsea or any of my other female relatives. Second of all, I saw how you looked at her earlier tonight and lastly, you just made sense about her and told me to back off. You're usually a rush-in-and-solve-problems kind of guy." Brian grabbed two beers and handed one to Rafe. Rafe cracked it open and took several long pulls before he answered.

"Well, Chelsea is eight months pregnant and married with two small kids. So not my type. No offense or anything." Rafe sobered a moment. "Would that be a problem? If I had some indefinable something for Belle?"

"Chelsea wouldn't have you. As for Belle? Depends on what you did, now, wouldn't it? Like say, if you used her for sex and hurt her? Yeah, that would be a problem, a big one. At the risk of sounding like a cliché, what are your intentions?"

Rafe took a deep breath before he said anything. She'd had his head swimming since that moment earlier when he'd sniffed her neck. "I don't quite know. I've been attracted to Belle for several years now. But we don't see each other more than a few times a year and in the last year or so, not even that. But tonight I kissed her. Things feel different. By the way, I don't use *anyone* for sex, asshole. But what I feel for Belle isn't casual. She's someone special to me and she has been for pretty much the entire time she's been alive. I know her. She knows me. I've never been attracted to someone I already had such an intimate relationship with before. It's intense and sort of scary. But the time is right, or at least it might be."

Brian put his hands over his ears theatrically a moment.

"Okay. That's enough. For now. Hell, maybe you can give her a reason to quit her job and move back to Davis. Slow down and work at a job that doesn't kill her. But please, for the love of all that is holy, if you...well, just keep it down. I'll turn on the fan so I can't hear anything." He shuddered and Rafe laughed.

"That's enough of that topic. Never fear, I have no desire to involve you in my romantic life."

They spoke for another half an hour or so, working through the oddness of Rafe and Belle possibly being an item. It was important to Rafe that Brian understood he'd never intentionally hurt Belle. Important to have his blessing in a sense and in the end, it felt like he had it.

"I have to be up at four-thirty tomorrow. I'm going to bed." He put his empty beer bottle in the recycle bin before nodding in Brian's direction and heading toward his room.

Belle had gone back to her room and changed. She'd brushed her teeth and gotten into bed and closed her eyes only to end up tossing and turning.

She'd wanted to think about Rafe but instead the scene at her office when she'd been leaving came back to her.

Everyone had known she had plans to leave early. She'd gone in way before dawn to tie up any loose ends and had promised her family she'd be home well before dinner that night.

"Annabelle, are you actually going to leave now?" David Pendergast, the lead attorney on the Morgan project, stood in her office doorway as she grabbed her things and made ready to finally get the heck out of there.

"It's already six, I've been here over twelve hours and I

promised my family I'd be at dinner by seven. I'm already going to be late." Belle looked him square in the face, knowing the situation demanded that sort of calm assertiveness. How depressing to think that even just leaving her office was like a PhD project in psychology.

He remained blocking her exit and she sighed inwardly.

"You really should rethink this vacation, Annabelle. It doesn't look right, a junior partner taking this much time off. You're at a very important point in your career."

Said the man who took three weeks in Aruba just two months before. He could kiss her booty because she wasn't going to make excuses for taking a mere fraction of her accrued vacation.

Belle smiled tightly and pushed her way past. "I'm aware of that. I need to go, David. Enjoy your ski trip. I'll see you next week."

He grabbed her arm and she looked up at him sharply, pulling back. "I think you've done a great job on this case, Annabelle, but you're needed here. You can't just hare off to bumfuck nowhere to play family for five days! No one but senior partners do that sort of thing."

She knew what this was really about. He'd hit on her repeatedly and she'd said no. He was married for goodness sake! And he was a butthead to boot.

"First of all, don't put your hand on me again. Let me be clear with you—I've put in my time and more. I lead in billable hours for this entire year. I'm at *double* the highest average for last year. Do you know what that means? I've been here eighty hours a week for pretty much this entire year. I have not had a single day off since January. I missed my mother's birthday. I missed my dad's birthday and my sister's baby shower. I am taking this time. Period. The project is finished. There are no motions left to file, the final judgment will come back in early January. Have a nice holiday." She narrowed her eyes at him. He sighed heavily and she darted past him quickly, heading toward the elevators.

"Don't cry to me when you don't get top pick of cases next month," he called out and she didn't let her breath out until the doors closed behind her and she headed away from the toxic pit her life had become.

As she finally got through town and headed east, the chest pains began to ease. This was so *not* how she'd envisioned her life would be after the back-breaking universe of law school and then clawing her way up and into a junior partner spot at Hansen, Petelman and Gruber.

Making matters worse, the freaking blowout had happened. She'd sat on the side of the road for ten minutes, finally giving in to tears she'd been saving up for many frustrated months.

No doubt about it, her life was a mess and she hated her job. The real question was what she would do.

"I should have sex with Rafe, that's what I should do." Instead, she got out of bed and began to make a list.

He heard her muttering and tapped on her door. When she opened it, she stood there tousled and holding a legal pad and three different colored pens.

"Hi."

"Hi there. You want to come in?" She stood back and he took the bottle of tequila and the shot glasses in with him.

"You look stressed. I say we do a few shots, make out a lot, you let me get to, oh say third base and we call it a night."

Her brow furrowed and the cutest little line etched between her eyes. "Really?"

"Belle Taylor, I know you're not offended. You get a totally different look on your face when you're offended. Why are you confused?" He put the bottle and glasses down before tossing himself on the bed.

She put the pad on the desk on the far side of the room and lined her pens up, horizontally, one by one, in a neat and orderly row. Then she exhaled and pursed the lips he knew tasted like heaven.

"I'm confused because you've always treated me like Brian's pesky little sister and tonight out of the blue you kiss me and then tease me and talk about sex and show up in my room and suggest third base!"

"I did indeed. I'd suggest more but I want to drag that out. At least for another day or so." He laughed, loving the way she snorted at him.

"I *could* use a drink. Move over. Jeez, you're a bed hog." She smoothed out the blankets before she sat. "What? No salt or lime?"

"If I had it, you could lick it off my belly." Wait, that wasn't a tease, that sounded just fine to him as a matter of fact.

"Well do you?" One of her regal eyebrows slid upward and her mouth struggled against a smile.

He sat up and filled both glasses with the tawny liquid. "Go on, you first. God knows you look like you could use it." He could too after her little tease.

She took the glass and drained it, her eyes watering a bit as she wiped her mouth on the back of her hand very uncharacteristically.

"Belle Taylor, did you just wipe tequila off your mouth with the back of your hand like, oh I don't know, like me?" He laughed before doing the same thing and refilling their glasses.

"When does the kissing start?" Her eyes widened and she quickly drained the next shot. "Crap, I can't even blame that on the alcohol yet."

"You want another?"

"Why not?"

Belle let the heat of the alcohol settle into her, bringing a languid fluidity to her muscles. She sighed and looked at the man in bed with her.

"You're really gorgeous, you know that?"

"I like it when you've been drinking, Belle." He winked and she snorted.

"Whatever. You were going to tell me why you're suddenly interested in my bases after giving me sweaters for Christmas for the last dozen years."

He grabbed her ankle and yanked, pulling her down as he rolled on top of her. Wow, he was good.

His mouth met hers, insistent, wet and hot. It was just the two of them, no worries about someone walking into the hallway. She let go of her control and gave in, sliding her hands up his arms, over his shoulders and into his hair. Soft, so soft and cool against her skin.

Heat licked at her insides when his tongue confidently invaded her mouth. When he rolled his hips, she moved, wrapping one of her calves around his ass, opening herself to him and holding him in place.

He broke the kiss, and looked into her face. "Just making sure you're still with me. I think about your bases a lot. I have for several years now. I told myself it was stupid to give in but you taste too good to resist. You're here, I'm here and we're both adults who know and like each other."

"I'm still with you, although you're not feeling me up or anything, which if I recall correctly, is part of the bases thing, right? And how long? God, you've wanted to kiss me and..." she shivered violently when he trailed fingertips up her belly, against her bare skin under her tee shirt, "...do that? You just kept it to yourself when I've like had the dirtiest fantasies ever about you?"

He tweaked a nipple then as he appeared to have to make a lot of effort to breathe.

"Christ, Belle, I can't believe you just told me you had dirty fantasies about me." He leaned down and sucked her nipple right through her tee shirt, leaving her no alternative but to hold on and enjoy it.

"I do. I did. All the time. You have no idea how good you look. Or crap, maybe you do. Should we get under the sheets?"

He laughed, breaking free of her nipple and looking at her again. "Honey, it's killing you to muss these blankets isn't it?"

"Well, the coverlet will get wrinkled and...oh my..." She lost her ability to think when he reached between them, into the waistband of her loose cotton pants and stroked over her pussy through her panties.

"You're so wet and hot I can feel you through your panties."

"Fuck the coverlet. Let me touch you! Why do you keep moving away?" she demanded.

"First things first. No fucking tonight. I want us to be totally sober when that happens so I can take my time and make you fuck drunk instead. I will make you come though because I have to see it. I'd invite you to sleep with me tonight but I have to be up at four-thirty and you need your rest. Tomorrow night you *will* tell me all your naughty fantasies though."

She blew out an exasperated sigh. "Whatever it takes to get

you to let me touch you."

He laughed and she thought he'd never looked sexier. Rolling away a moment, he pulled off his jeans and shorts while she made quick work of her clothes too. When he turned back to her he groaned.

"Belle, you're beautiful. A glorious invitation to sin right there wrapped in velvety pale skin." As he moved to touch her, they both gasped at the shock of pleasure from bare skin meeting bare skin.

His mouth touched every part of her. The spot just below her ear, the hollow of her throat, the sensitive skin just beneath her breasts, her nipples, the backs of her knees. All the while, his hands touched wherever his mouth didn't.

But he wouldn't let her do much other than receive pleasure. "No, Belle, if you touch me I won't last. Please, let me love you." A lock of hair fell over his forehead, obscuring his right eye.

She managed a shaky nod, needing him so ridiculously bad she couldn't speak. However, that was nothing compared to the way it felt when he slid down between her thighs and shouldered them wide open.

Belle watched, fascinated by the way he drew his tongue over the seam where thigh met body. He stopped, breathing her in and she knew somewhere in the back of her mind she should be embarrassed but all she felt was utterly turned on and wildly flattered by the possessive action.

And then his mouth was on her pussy and she fell back against the pillows with a gurgled gasp of pleasure. Over and over, his tongue flicked, licked and teased every inch of her pussy until she thought she'd explode.

Her nipples throbbed, her skin tingled, her toes pointed and still he drove her relentlessly higher. He devoured her with avarice, devastated her with the way he seemed to crave her cunt. No one had ever gone down on her like this.

Finally, he drew her clit between his lips, gently scraping his teeth over it while at the same time sliding three fingers into her gate. It was too much and she lost it, falling hard into an incredibly intense orgasm.

Chapter Three

Belle awoke with a headache but still, all in all, felt very good. Until she remembered the night before and realized she'd come and fallen asleep without taking care of Rafe.

"Ugh. Selfish!" A glance at the clock told her it was already eight-thirty and she needed to be at her parents' house in half an hour. "Yikes!" Rolling out of bed, she saw the thermo-carafe of coffee and a note from Rafe.

With a smile, she poured herself a cup and headed toward the bathroom while reading.

If I know you, and I do, you're feeling guilty about last night. Don't. You have no idea how much I enjoyed it. I'll tell you, in detail, when we're alone next. You can make it up to me later on. We have time. I had to get out of here early. Hope the coffee is still hot. I'll see you tonight.

Rafe

PS. Your tire situation should be taken care of well before you have to leave this morning. Brian and Scott arranged for it first thing.

Wow. She jumped in the shower still smiling and clutching her coffee. Being taken care of felt very good and being with

Rafe felt very right. Scarily so.

Her mother waited for **her** as she walked into the house wearing a grin and feeling **more** relaxed than she had in ages.

"Good morning, Belle. **My,** you look pretty today. I take it you got a good night's rest **last** night. Sit down with Chelsea and I'll bring out breakfast." **Her** mother shoved her toward the kitchen table and she grabbed a mug for her coffee on her way.

Dropping a kiss on her sister's cheek, Belle slid into a chair and poured a cup of coffee from the carafe on the table. "Good morning, how're you?"

"Just gestating. You?"

"I am so ready to brave the hordes and shop today. Even the insanity of shopping four days before Christmas isn't enough to stop me. I haven't shopped in so long. Is Nana coming?"

Her mother chose that moment to slide a plate heaping with food before her and another in front of Chelsea.

"Mom! There has to be an entire pig on this plate."

"Don't argue with your mother. Eat." Brian strolled into the room.

"I totally chose the wrong profession. Doctors seem to have a lot of free time to hang out and freeload off their parents. By the way, thanks for taking care of my tire, loser."

Brian passed her the hot sauce for her eggs and potatoes and poured himself some coffee. "Don't hate, Annabelle. We can't all be brilliant."

"Yeah, so you became a doctor and Belle a lawyer. Leaving all the brilliance to me," Chelsea said around a mouthful of potatoes.

Chelsea *was* brilliant. Her weavings were works of art and she sold them as such. They hung on walls and were used on beds and other places all over the west. Her husband ran an art gallery and turned out to be a really clever business manager so Chels was able to stay at home with their children and still create art.

"Your grandmother is meeting us for lunch. She wanted to stay here with the kids this morning. Right now they're out with your dad and Kevin. Gabe Bettencourt promised a tour of the dairy later in the week, they're in heaven. And don't think I didn't notice you trying to put that bacon on your brother's plate, Belle. Eat it."

No one messed with Rita Taylor. The former Miss New Jersey had met Gil Taylor when they'd been nineteen and she'd been visiting Sacramento and that's all there'd been to it. She'd transferred to UC Davis and had finished school while Gil had worked his family's farm. They'd married when she graduated and had Brian within a few years and the rest of them had followed. She ruled the family with an iron fist, being the disciplinarian while their father had been the big softie. Belle got her ambition from her mother, along with her drive and her unending will to succeed.

By the time they got out of the house, Belle was pleasantly full and ready for the day. "Do you want me to drive?"

Her mother just rolled her eyes. "We're taking the van. Your car is too low for me."

"That and she can't be in charge in your car," Chelsea said in an undertone, making Belle laugh. Something else she got from her mother, she supposed.

They stopped off at a few smaller, family-run shops before heading to the mall. It was a good thing she'd earned a great bonus this year! It was also a good thing her mom had driven the van or all the loot wouldn't have fit in her BMW's trunk.

Then on to meet her grandmother for lunch. Where sadly, Nana pelted her relentlessly with questions about her life, her lack of a significant other, her long hours and her general state of *not quite good enough for all that schooling you had, missy.*

Belle adored her grandmother but she wasn't disappointed when her grandfather showed up to escort her grandmother to the salon to get her hair done.

Her mother heaved a big sigh when they walked into a pretty quiet house to wrap the presents.

"God, I need a drink after that. I'll make the Irish coffee and you two get the room set up to wrap." Her mother headed into the kitchen and the sisters dragged the bags and packages into the master bedroom.

Belle pointed at Chelsea. "You, out for a few minutes. Let me wrap yours and Mom's stuff and I'll call you when I'm done."

"Yeah and I have to pee anyway." Chelsea waved her away and headed out as Belle closed the door behind her. She found the things she'd picked up for her mom and sister and wrapped them quickly, finishing right as her mother barged in.

"Have a coffee. Poor Chels has to have decaf and no whiskey but you and I can have the good stuff."

"Nana is a wee bit hopped up today," Chelsea said, returning to the room. She began to pull out her own bags and packages to wrap and their mother did the same.

"A wee bit? Girls, I love my mother-in-law with all my heart, she's been good to me since the day I met her but I was overjoyed when they decided to live in Florida. I'm sorry, Belle. She means well. She does." Her mother took another several sips of the heavily laced coffee.

"I know she does." And her grandmother hadn't been

wrong. Not really. What good was that gorgeous condo overlooking the water when she was never home to enjoy the view? It hadn't been that hard to move to San Francisco for her job, after all it was only an hour away from Davis. But in truth, it wasn't the city that was the problem, it was the job. Or rather, the expectations.

"And um, jeez, Belle, you overdid it a bit." Chelsea indicated the heaps of loot Belle had bought.

"I didn't. I had a good year. What's the point of working eighty-hour weeks if I can't share the benefits of that with my family? I missed being here for a lot of stuff."

"We don't want your presents, Belle. We want *you*." Chelsea hugged her. "You're not happy. I've never seen you *not* wanting to check your phone, not wanting to talk about your job. Not ever. Even when you worked at Swenson's in high school you wanted to tell me about your work." Her sister again indicated all the stuff waiting to be wrapped. "A sweater, a train set, it's not a substitute for *you*. You're precious to us. Not your stuff. Not how much you make."

"I'm sorry, okay? You think I like it that I don't see you all?" Belle attempted to focus on how her sister just haphazardly cut the wrap and slapped tape on the package. It helped clear her mind as she made her own precise cuts and taped the paper correctly, making the package look its best. And it held back the frustrated tears too.

"You think we like not seeing you? For what, Belle? What is worth missing your sister's baby shower? I don't want to make you feel bad like Nana did. I am so proud of you. You're committed and dedicated and I know you're a smashing attorney. But at what cost? You can't tell me other attorneys all work this sort of schedule." Her mother sighed and began to wrap.

"You're like a ghost," Chelsea said softly. "You have always been such a huge part of this family. Making charts for who sits where at every holiday. Color coded cards for parties and meal planning. You iron pillowcases and tea towels. When you're not around, well, there's a Belle-sized hole in the world and it sucks."

Belle sat on the floor next to the bed and put her head in her hands. "I've been alone you know? I work my ass off every day. I get up before sunrise, I get home way after dark. I work. That's all I do. But if I want that corner office, if I want what I've always wanted, that's the cost."

"This isn't supposed to evoke guilt. I respect your drive and your dreams but I don't want to lose a child over it. There has to be another way." Her mother sat next to her.

"I don't know. I need to think and break it all down. Right now, we need to wrap presents and then I have to head over to the Bettencourts to get some milk and butter for baking, remember?"

They continued to wrap, joined, on and off, by other relatives who showed up. Kevin came in and hauled presents out to the tree and the boys came in with Belle's dad, rambunctious and demanding cookies.

"I'll run over to the dairy and take them with me. Two birds and all that."

"Bless you," Chelsea said from her perch on the bed.

Admittedly, it was selfish of her too. She had to get away for a bit and she also wanted to see Rafe. It wasn't like she thought the night before meant they were getting married, but she'd had a crush on the man from a pretty young age. Having sex with him—or third base and if it was third base, the kids were really wild these days—was really amazing. But more than that, it was him seeing her as a woman, in a way she'd lain in her bed at night, hands clasped, begging in her prayers for that blew her away so much.

Suddenly she felt more alive than she had in a long time. She still needed to deal with her job, but for a while, she could be a fun, sexy woman sleeping with a man she loved and trusted. The wonderful normalcy of that, while still being totally hot was just awesome and giddy making.

The boys chattered in the back seat and got all excited when they turned up the long drive leading to the dairy offices and their small retail store. Once she'd parked and they got out, the boys ran toward the fences nearby where the milk was pasteurized, homogenized and bottled for transport. Rafe and Gabriel, Rafe's oldest brother, had convinced their father and two other brothers to switch over to organic feed and no hormones or antibiotics for the cows. They'd lost money for two years but ever since had been turning a decent profit. Rafe's dedication to organic farming was really sexy. Well, everything about him was really sexy but a man with a passion about something important was something Belle found alluring.

"Belle Taylor! Honey, how are you?" Beatriz Bettencourt saw Belle and drew her into a hug. "It's so good to see you. Raphael told us you were coming home for the holidays. You'll have to come over tomorrow for lunch. *Sopas.* I'm making it today. And several loaves of bread since I knew you'd be here."

Portuguese sweetbread was heaven and Belle loved it. Add the fresh butter they made there on site and a cup of hot coffee and you had yourself heaven. And *sopas*, the rich, tasty soup with *coives*, or greens, usually kale, potatoes and hunks of beef so tender they fell apart, spiced just right, was another favorite of Belle's.

"You are an angel of heaven and I adore you, Mrs.

Bettencourt. It's great to see you too. And I'd love to come to lunch tomorrow. Thank you for inviting me. You know I'd never want to miss *sopas* and sweet bread."

"I thought I saw a beautiful woman. Belle Taylor, you're a sight for very tired eyes." Gabriel Bettencourt came in and hugged her, kissing her cheek. "Rafe said you were here. What brings you out? Not that I'm complaining mind you. You're much nicer to look at than cows."

"Flatterer. Or, I think so anyway." Belle laughed. "I'm here for some milk and butter. We're making cookies and bread. And the boys would love a tour at some point before they go back to LA."

"I thought that was Chelsea's van outside. But look here, even better than a pregnant woman married to someone else, I get a single one I fancy more than a little bit." Rafe walked right over to her and kissed her square on the mouth, surprising and pleasing her even as she didn't know what else to think about the public declaration of affection.

"Hello there, Annabelle. What brings you out here?" He smiled as he drew his thumb down her jawline. He was dusty and smelled of hay and fresh, cool air and she had to stifle the urge to rub her hands all over him.

"Um, well, hello to you too. I'm here to get milk and butter, we're baking this afternoon and the boys wanted to see the dairy so I thought I'd bring them along."

"Belle is coming to lunch tomorrow, Raphael." Beatriz looked at Belle with undisguised interest, in a way she'd never looked at her before.

"That's a very fine idea. Since she's staying in my guest room I'll drive her over. All right with you, Belle?" Rafe had a sparkle in his eyes Belle guessed had something to do with the guest room comment.

"Sure. Thanks."

"And bring the kids back a day or two after Christmas. Rosemary and her family are coming so we can get the boys a tour of the dairy and they'll have kids their age to play with." Gabe spoke with one eyebrow slightly raised. He lazily shifted his gaze to his brother for a moment and back to Belle.

Before Belle could reply the boys were jumping up and down happily agreeing.

Belle grinned. "That'd be great. Thanks, Gabe." She looked back to the boys. "Now, let's get this stuff back home or your grandma is going to tan my hide. Sugar cookies from Rita Taylor's kitchen are a big task and I know she needs your help." And Belle didn't know what else to do or say to Rafe and his family right then. Clearly last night meant something to him, more than just a quick roll in the proverbial hay.

But what she hadn't been ready for was how much the idea pleased her. Which in turn scared the bejesus out of her.

"I'll walk you to your car then, help you carry the stuff." Rafe grabbed the box with the milk and butter and led the way.

Belle waved back over her shoulder, thanking Mrs. Bettencourt and telling them she'd see them the following afternoon.

Rafe loaded the stuff into the van and went to Belle's window, leaning in to steal another kiss from her. He liked how she'd responded, not pulling back or showing embarrassment.

"I'll see you when you get home tonight."

"Okay." Her voice was a bit breathless, her pupils nearly swallowed the irises of her eyes and he found he rather liked the effect he had on Ms. Annabelle Taylor, Esquire. "I'll bring you some cookies."

"Mmm, cookies. Thank you, Belle."

He watched her drive off and wanted to laugh at the look she'd had on her face. Consternation. He'd flustered the unflappable Annabelle Taylor and from what he'd seen since they'd found her on the side of the road the night before, she needed a lot more unflapping. She may be a total control freak but in bed she was on fire and marvelously inventive. He'd have to see just what else she had in store for him.

"Mind telling me why you kissed Annabelle Taylor like she was way more than your best friend's little sister?" Gabe asked lazily as he came to stand next to Rafe.

"Gabe, I think I fell in love with Belle a long time ago, only my common sense blew me off and reminded me she had more in her future than a dusty farmer-slash-dairyman. She still deserves that but damned if my common sense isn't currently being pummeled by my heart."

"Love? What the hell are you talking about?" Gabe's easy stance straightened as he turned to face his brother fully.

"I've always loved Belle like family. I've liked her, respected her, admired her drive, even if I've often thought she was too stiff and a control freak. But she was indeed, Brian's baby sister and in that way, she was like Rosemary to me. But at that big party they had out at the farm when she graduated from law school? I don't know, I just looked up and saw her and she wasn't like a sister anymore. She was a woman and all the love I'd had for her was still there, only different. Better because I've known her forever and I know she's good and kind and thinks family is important like I do. She's a girl from a farm, even with a suit on, she's still one of us and she's not ashamed of it." Rafe kicked the dirt a moment.

"And the kiss?"

Rafe gave him a general update on the kiss and brief

overview of the night before. "I think I realized, the first moment I, um, yeah, anyway, I think I realized this morning when I was operating on a few hours of sleep and wanted to be sure her tire was okay, just how much I want Belle the woman. I know her and that's special. I want something with her."

"But?" Gabe always had read him well.

"But she has dreams, Gabe. You know how she is. Even when she was like eight or nine she had these freaking flowchart things for every little decision in her life. She wants the letterhead and the office and I want that for her. But I don't know if there's room for me *and* for that."

"I take it you haven't spoken to her about any of this."

"I've been thinking about it all day. I just came to the decision to pursue her for real only about two hours ago. It's one thing to want her, it's another thing to go after it for real. I had to mull it over and think on it."

Gabe slapped his shoulder and laughed. "Mom saw that kiss. She loves Belle, she loves the Taylors. She'll make sweetbread until Belle is so fat she can't fit in her car to leave town if she has to. Hell, Mom would be happy with anyone other than Sarah." His brother snorted at the mention of Rafe's ex. "But Belle is family already and I have no doubt Mom's in there right now planning her little heart out."

"Good. I fight dirty, Gabe. I want Belle Taylor and I'm willing to share her with a job she loves and deserves. But I think she deserves more than what she's got. I think she knows it too." Rafe shoved his hands in his pockets. "I have to go clean up. I'll be back in an hour or so."

Rafe drove the short trip to his house and thought of Belle. Thought of the way she'd been the night before. Of her taste and the sounds she made as she came. Of the passion in her eyes and the way she'd touched him. Of her revelation that she'd had a crush on him for ages. He'd known of course, that she looked up to him when she'd been younger and yeah, he'd caught a few of those fifteen-year-old moony faces but he hadn't given it much thought. He was four years older than her so she'd not been on his radar at the time. Even the way his heart had felt when she'd fallen into sleep after he'd gone down on her. Protective. Satisfied *he'd* been the one to relax her and help her rest.

Still, the idea that she'd had teenaged fantasies about him really turned him on. They'd have to explore that one in detail. In the meantime, he needed to go home, shower and change to get rid of the smell of the dairy before he went back over to his parents' for dinner.

Chapter Four

Belle sat, her legs tucked beneath her, and looked at the long garland of dried apple slices and cranberries her nephews, aided by her father, had hung on the tree. She'd made garlands like this for the Taylor Christmas tree since she was three and the act of doing it every year, of that ritual, calmed and comforted her.

The house smelled like cookies and fresh pine, Nat King Cole sang Christmas carols in the background and all was right with the world exactly in that moment.

How she'd missed this kind of thing! Her family had done this without her for the other holidays and birthdays and the idea made her stomach clench. On one hand, she was happy they had each other but on the other, she wasn't there to share it and it happened anyway.

"Want some more gingerbread?" Scott held the plate in her direction, making her groan.

"I will burst apart and make a mess if I eat another bite. I need to go running tomorrow, I think, or I'll gain fifteen pounds before I go back to work."

She knew he wanted to say something but he simply snorted and left it at that.

"I'm actually going to head on back to Brian's. I'm tired and since we'll be doing the big decorating stuff tomorrow night, I need my rest." She stood and kissed everyone before heading out.

"I'll be home in a bit, I need to stop over at the hospital to check on one of my patients," Brian called out.

"Tell Rafe we expect him for dinner if he's not having it at his parents' tomorrow," her mother absently said as she wrapped up a platter of goodies Belle had promised to bring home to him.

"I'm having lunch over there tomorrow, by the way. But if he's home when I get there, I'll tell him." Belle did her best to sound nonchalant about him but knew she failed.

Her mother's eyes came to rest on her, razor sharp and not missing the sound of Belle's voice. "I'll walk you out."

Crap, she was in for it.

"So...anything you want to tell me before I start getting phone calls?" Her mother stood in the path of her car door, preventing her from making a quick getaway.

"About what?" Belle put the platter of baked goods on the passenger seat and tried not to look directly at her mother.

"Annabelle Louise Taylor, don't you try that with me, young lady. You know what."

She sighed. "I'm not sure, to be totally honest with you. But in some way, Rafe and I are involved. Other than that basic thing, I don't know. I don't know what it means, what it is, what he thinks about it. It was unexpected. How did you know, anyway?"

"Good Lord, Belle, do you think I'm an idiot? I raised five children, one of them being Kevin! I know all sorts of things based on what they say and how they say it. Your voice when you said you were going to lunch and then if you'd see him tonight, it changed, softened and your eyes lit up. I suppose that's why you had such a bounce in your step this morning?"

"All right, this is officially making me uncomfortable. I'm going to go now. I'll see you tomorrow. I love you." Belle tugged on her door and her mother made a show of slooooowly moving out of the way.

"I expect to hear more about this. I like Rafe. He's a good man and he's part of our family already. You can count on a man like him."

"He *is* a good man. I've liked Rafe a very long time and I'll talk to you later." Belle closed her door firmly, locked it and drove away.

He *was* a good man. Handsome. Solid. He believed in things, made a difference, was committed to his family and community. That was rare. And he was hot in bed.

His truck was in the driveway and the lights blazed in the house. Her heartbeat quickened once she knew he was there.

When she walked into the large living room, she caught sight of him stretched out, long legs propped up on a side table, watching television. But when he heard her, he turned, giving her all his attention and the look he gave her nearly knocked her to her knees.

"I brought you some cookies and gingerbread. My mother said you need to try the new shortbread recipe and tell her what you think."

He stood without saying anything and stalked to her. Her heart thundered in her chest as he took the platter and put it down. One of his arms banded around her waist and pulled her close while his mouth sought hers, capturing it, taking and giving.

Pleasure unfurled low in her gut and drifted outward until she was lazy with it, warm and nearly purring.

Giving in, she relaxed into his body as she wrapped herself around him, needing to touch him. Her hands greedily slid through his hair and down the muscles of his neck, so hard and strong. Heat from his body buffeted her, wrapping her in his scent and presence.

His tongue lazily stroked along hers, sending his taste spiraling through her. The kiss seemed so laid back on the surface but his arm held her to him tight and his cock pressed into her belly. When she nipped his bottom lip between her teeth he groaned.

Her nipples stabbed the front of her sweater, her pussy slickened and bloomed. A low throb of need settled in tandem between nipples and clit and she realized he'd taken her to nearly begging with just a kiss.

"You taste like spiced cider," he said against her lips as he broke the kiss. "I like it." His tongue slid over her lips and the act sent a burst of giddiness through her.

She paused, looking for the flirty banter to return his with. "I have nothing at all. Sorry. You're way better at this than I am." She had to tip her head back to see him better.

"You have everything, Belle. But thank you. How was dinner?" He drew her back to his chair and settled her into his lap facing him.

"It was good. We wrapped what seemed like three thousand presents, did the garlands, baked cookies, frosted them, made colored sugar. Brian's new girlfriend stopped by for a few minutes to drop off presents and suggested very brightly that we all go sing carols. I sort of felt sorry for her because you'd think my family would be all over that sort of thing but I get the feeling they don't like her much. How was your dinner?"

"Wow, did you even take a breath?" He laughed. "No, I don't think Sissy is much liked by your family. She's too young for

Brian and everyone can see it but him. She tries too hard and it only makes people want to avoid her more." He kissed her quickly and she snuggled into him. "Dinner was good. Mom is baking like a fiend, my dad is just staying out of the way. Gabriel snuck off to meet someone, he's playing it close to the vest. My mother asked me pointed questions about you."

"Me?"

Rafe loved the way her voice squeaked when she asked. Loved the look of worry and also pleasure on her face.

"Yes, you. And us. She didn't miss the kiss this afternoon of course. She loves you, always has." He wanted to tell her he loved her too but he was still unsure about how to approach the situation. He didn't want to scare her away or make her feel like she had to choose. At the moment he thought it might be the best strategy to let her know he was interested in a relationship but not push overly hard. Then he'd do everything he could to remind her why having a job where you didn't work eighty hours a week and be away from your family for a year at a time was a good thing.

"My mom cornered me in the driveway."

Mrs. Taylor always had been a very astute woman. "Oh yeah? Did she catch you writing a note asking Gabe to ask me if I *liked* you liked you but not to say you were asking?"

The way she blushed and coughed made him realize her crush on him had been a pretty big one. He grinned as he stood, still holding her.

"Let's get somewhere private. Brian may walk in and that would really just kill my libido."

She nodded eagerly and wrapped her legs around his waist as he carried her up the stairs and into his room. Once the door was closed and locked he tossed her on the bed. She

151

immediately smoothed the blankets and he laughed, remembering he'd forgotten to make it that morning.

"So, Belle, I get the feeling I starred in lots of teenaged fantasies and I didn't even know it. I was a lot older so I was blind but I find the idea of you writing my name on your folder quite interesting. What did you think about me?"

She blushed again and he used the remote to turn the stereo on. He switched off the overhead light and instead used the small bedside lamps.

He wondered if she'd tell him but she surprised him when she got to her knees and sat back on her haunches, her hands clasped on her thighs.

"I was young, you know, when I first started crushing on you. It was like at fifteen when it became something real. Even so my fantasies about you usually involved a lot of tongue kissing and you taking me places and other people seeing Rafe Bettencourt was my date. I knew about sex and all, but I hadn't had it so that part was sort of murky. Later though, when I was older, that wasn't so murky."

His cock twitched at the way she wet her lips nervously.

"Go on."

"Take off your shirt." She tipped her chin in his direction.

Random. Okay, it was one step closer to naked anyway so it's not like he suffered or anything.

She looked him over once he'd removed his shirt and sighed. "I remember once, right after I got my license, I had to drive over to the dairy to drop something off for your mom and you were playing hoops in the driveway with the guys. You were obviously the skins. So I sat in my car for like five minutes in the boiling heat, watching you all sweaty and shirtless playing basketball. I thought I'd die at how sexy you looked and I never wanted anything more than I wanted you to notice me right then. Only Brian teased me about something when he saw me and you looked at me the same way Brian had." Her voice was wistful and he reached up to pull her hair free of the braid she'd captured it in.

"Did you ever masturbate when you thought of me?" he asked, his voice loud in the quiet of the room.

Her breath caught and a wave of desire so strong his own breath caught rolled over him at the realization she had.

Slowly, she nodded and he swallowed. "When you were younger?"

"Yes, then. But last month too." She criss-crossed her arms and pulled her sweater up and over her head. Her small breasts were free of a bra and he leaned in to drop a kiss on each nipple. When he sat back she squirmed out of her pants and the black lacy panties before laying back and continuing to look up at him.

The balance had shifted and suddenly she had control again. He raised a single brow in her direction. Her answer was to trail her fingers up her belly and around her nipples.

"You're doing that on purpose." He nearly panted as he watched her.

"Genius deduction." She quirked up a smile and caught her bottom lip between her teeth for a moment.

He liked this lighter side of her. He knew she had a sense of humor, had seen it many times as they grew up, but he'd never imagined this woman behind the suit existed. Teasing, sexy, in charge without being a control freak.

"So you were about to masturbate for me while telling me what you fantasize about while doing it."

"I was? Hmm, well, perhaps if you do it too. I'm shy."

He barked a laugh. "Anal retentive? Yes. Shy? Not even."

"I am not anal retentive. I am detail oriented!" Her eyes sparked and he sobered. Sort of.

"Annabelle, at the risk of sidetracking what has been a very promising interlude, you are the most anal retentive person I've ever met. You have your shoes arranged according to season, color and heel height. Who does that? You have a thing about eating food, I've watched you! You eat one bite of each thing in a very precise order with timed sips of beverage. Even the way you cut your meat is like a feat of modern engineering."

"How do you know about my shoes?" she demanded, still looking hotter than the sun as her breasts heaved with indignation. "And anyway, it's easy to find what you need when you're organized. I'm organized, not anal!"

"The shoe story is an old one, everyone who knows you and your family knows about your shoes, honey. They also know you iron tea towels and anyone who's ever been with you when you put flowers into a vase knows about how *organized* you are."

"What's that supposed to mean?" Her eyes widened and he responded by unzipping his jeans. The haughtier she became, the more he wanted to fuck her.

"Belle, you take half an hour to arrange the flowers. Most people just plunk them into water and enjoy them." Off came the jeans and his boxers.

"You can enjoy them more if they're arranged in some semblance of order. If the shorter flowers are in the center you can't see them. Where's the enjoyment in that?" Her breath came out in a huff as he leaned down and bit a nipple.

"I love your tits. Probably because you rarely wear a bra and they're free beneath those silky shirt things you wear beneath your sweaters and stuff. Sometimes I just watch you to catch sight of a jiggle. And then I come home and jerk off thinking about that. I've got it bad, Belle." He fought a grin but she didn't win her battle and even threw in an eye roll as she snickered.

"They're very small. I wear bras at work of course. I can't very well *jiggle* around my co-workers. And you're changing the subject." She moaned softly as he sucked a nipple into his mouth, gentle at first and then harder until she jerked, her nails digging into his biceps to hold him in place.

When he'd had his fill, for the moment, he pulled back so he could see her face again. "They're beautiful. Beauty isn't about size. They fit you, they're just right for your body."

"So, you watched my boobs and masturbated? When? You know, Rafe, it would have been nice if you'd told me about this a few years ago. Do you know how frustrated I am when I get home from visits here?"

"The sway of these luscious little beauties would make my cock so damned hard it made me want to hit something. I'd spend all day long thinking about what color your nipples were, what shape and then by the time I got home I'd have to head straight for the shower. When you didn't come here at all this year, I missed you, even if nothing happened between us, I missed you. Now," he settled on the bed, facing her, "I think you should tell me about what you thought about and show me how you touch yourself."

"Do you want the fifteen-year-old version or the twenty-eight-year-old version? They're very different. For instance, when I was younger, I used to think about you coming into my room, late at night after you and Brian had gotten back from wherever the heck you two got off to. You'd sneak in and crawl over me, kiss me to wake me up." Her legs parted and she slipped one hand between them while the other palmed a nipple.

He watched, ensnared as she wet her fingers in her mouth and traced them around a glistening nipple.

"And the last time you..."

"Fingered myself?"

He nearly choked. "Honey, there's a naughty girl inside you, isn't there?"

She nodded slowly. "Woman. I haven't been a girl in a very long time. But to answer your question, yes. The last time I used you to make myself come, I was in my shower. God, after a fifteen-hour day. I have a waterproof vibrator and I soaped myself up, thinking of you, thinking of your hands all over me."

She arched, widening her thighs and he saw the evidence of just how naughty she was.

"Go on." He closed a fist around his cock, stroking slowly as he watched one of her hands move down her belly. Her eyes locked with his as she spread her labia open, leaving her middle finger free. His entire body froze as her finger disappeared inside her pussy and pulled free, slick with her honey.

Her voice caught as she began to tease her clit. "I have no willpower when it comes to orgasms, Rafe," she whispered. "I always wish I could tease myself but I never can wait. I thought about you bending me forward, putting my hands on the tile, moving my feet apart and slamming your cock into my cunt, hard. I'd want to play with my nipples but I had to hold on because you fuck into me so hard. But I'm whimpering..." And she whimpered a moment, a sound laced with need as she sped her movement on her clit, her hips churning.

"Christ, Belle." His balls crawled up close to his body and he had to let go of his cock or he'd blow.

"You reach around and touch my clit while you fuck me. You say the most incredible things in my ear and when I start to come, you only thrust harder because my pussy is grabbing you, making you hot, pushing you to come with me."

Her eyes fluttered closed and she pinched her nipple harder as the muscles in her wrist corded while she worked her clit. A charming, sexy flush swam up her body from the tips of her French manicured toes to her gorgeous tits. She blew out a breath and a long moan as she came.

Her scent flooded his senses and unable to resist, he grabbed her wrist and brought her fingers to his mouth, licking them as she watched, her lips parted.

"Well now, Belle Taylor, you're a big surprise, aren't you?"

She smiled slow and sexy and flopped back to the mattress. "I guess so."

Belle looked her fill at him, still kneeling above her. He was unbelievably perfect, her fantasy come true. Never before had she freed all the stuff reeling through her head during sex. Sure she organized her shoes by heel height but she preferred sex raw and for want of a better word, dirty. But she rarely got it that way because the men she ended up with saw her outward control and calm and thought she'd be the same way in bed.

"Whatever are you thinking about, Belle?" The smile that took the corner of his mouth made her wet all over again.

"You were going to tell me about what you think about while getting yourself off."

"Ah, just so."

"But I want you here, straddling me. I want to see it close up." She indicated where she wanted him and he shrugged, moving and settling over her upper thighs, the heat of his balls resting against her mound.

"I can feel how wet your pussy is against my balls. Jesus." She watched the up and down movement of his Adam's apple before he went on. "I love the way you move. So precise. Most people just bumble through life but you, Belle, you always move like you have a plan. That's so sexy. But underneath that military precision, there's that sway of those juicy little breasts. I think about what it feels like when the soft cotton of your shirt brushes over your nipples. Does it turn you on? I wondered how sensitive they were. What they tasted like."

He took his cock in his fist and slowly began to stroke himself, never taking his eyes from hers.

"I'd find you outside, it would be late summer. The night would be that sort of purple just before dark fell fully. It'd be quiet, air would be sweet from the trees, we'd hear buzzing bees and the sound of water. I'd approach you from behind and slowly take off your shirt and I'd finally see your breasts. I'd lay you down and...fuck this." Rafe moved down her body, pushing her thighs apart. "I don't need to tell you my damned fantasy, you're here, naked and your scent is making me crazy. You are my fantasy come true, Belle."

Feeling ridiculously pleased, she watched as he grabbed a condom and rolled it on. She reached down and spread her pussy open for him, waiting.

"Damn it, you're so fucking sexy," he muttered as he wasted no more time and began to press into her body with his cock, spreading her body apart as he filled her completely.

She allowed her eyes to droop as the exquisite sensation of being impaled on his cock settled into her system. He was nice and thick and it'd been eight months since she'd had sex with anyone not silicone. He hissed as she moaned, shifting her thighs up, angling her hips to take him deeper.

"This first time, I want to be face to face, but later, I'm going to fuck you from behind. Maybe in the shower with your hands on the tiles."

Her breath caught as a flash of her fantasy came to her.

Only he was real. Hard and real and buried deep in her body.

She caressed every inch of him she could reach while matching his rhythm, rolling her hips to meet his strokes. There was no sound but them, the slick sound of body meeting body, of breath and the rustling of sheets. But inside, Belle's body sang, her heart sang even though she was scared as hell of the enormity of what she felt for him at that moment. So much tenderness in his eyes.

Still watching her face, he leaned on one arm to move his free hand between them. He brought his fingertips down where they were joined to gather her honey and slick the way around her clit.

A shock of intense pleasure hit her at that first contact and echoed over and over as his fingers continued to play over her clit. When her climax hit, it pulled her under as she held on to his ass, her fingers digging into the solid muscle. She had no words, just a long gasping sigh.

Long moments later he pressed a kiss to her forehead, got out of bed and came back quickly.

"That was amazing, Belle," he said quietly, kissing her again, this time on the lips.

"It was. It feels sort of unreal. I mean, last night was one thing. Oh and I'm sorry I fell asleep, God, how rude!" She blushed but be laughed.

"Belle, you had dark circles under your eyes. They're not nearly as bad today. You know how I felt when I saw you'd fallen asleep?"

She shook her head.

"Good. Accomplished. I'd taken care of you and helped you rest. I *liked* that."

She smiled, shifting a bit on the blankets.

"It's the sheets and blankets being mussed up, isn't it?"

"Oh okay, yes! It makes everything all wrinkled and don't you make your bed in the mornings? It's so much nicer to crawl between sheets of a made bed."

He laughed until tears ran from his eyes while she glared. "Belle, you're one of a kind."

She shoved him out of bed and stood, tightening his sheets, re-tucking them and straightening the blankets before pulling them back to expose the sheets. "Now, get in."

He grabbed her and brought her down with him. "Thank you. You're right, it does feel better."

She rolled over his body so he was on the side closest to the door. "That's better. I like this side."

"You're lucky I'm easy and I find it totally sexy when you're all anal."

She cocked her head. "You're lucky I'm easy and fingered my pussy while you watched." Satisfaction settled into her when she saw his eyes flare with heat and how he had to make an effort to take a deep breath.

"You're absolutely right. Will you sleep with me tonight? I have to be up early but I won't even turn the alarm on, I have an internal clock."

"Yeah." She snuggled into his body, breathing him in. He smelled so damned good and when he put his arms around her, she felt totally right.

"You want to talk to me about your job?"

"Rafe Bettencourt, I feel all relaxed and warm. It's heaven and I don't think I've felt this good in years and years. No, I don't want to even think about it right now."

"Would you bop me on the head with a pillow if I woke you up to fuck you in a few hours?" He nudged her ass with his cock when she turned and backed into the curve of his body.

"I'll bop you if you don't. Now shut up. You've made me very tired and I have to get some beauty rest. It's tree trimming day tomorrow and then lunch with your family and then dinner with mine. My aunt, uncle and cousins should arrive before dinner. My mother said to invite you if you're not busy with your family."

"Am I allowed to answer or will you bop me? You scare me, Belle. You've got that dominatrix thing going for you. Although that doesn't so much scare me as make me want to have sex with you." He chuckled. "Rosemary and the kids won't be in until tomorrow so I can definitely come by at least for some of your mom's stellar dessert."

"Good. I like to look at you."

Chapter Five

Rafe liked to look at her too. He watched her as she helped his mother in the large kitchen, slicing tomatoes for the salad with engineer-like precision. She did it quickly and efficiently and yet he bet every single slice was perfectly the same size.

She'd not protested when he hugged and kissed her when they walked into the house. He'd simply acted like she was his and to his great relief, she simply was his.

Her outfit was pretty and feminine, although he was convinced the pleat on the front of her soft blue pants was sharp enough to slice paper. Funny, he wouldn't have found another woman dressed the same way sexy but that shirt buttoned up, just exposing the hollow of her throat, made him want to lick her. She exuded such a softness despite the spine of steel, the contradiction fascinated him.

Lunch was good. His mother's attitude toward Belle had shifted from that of a family friend to that of a potential mother-in-law. She wasn't just Belle Taylor, she was Belle and Rafe. He wondered if she caught that. He doubted she missed it, his woman was intelligent in addition to sexy.

When Belle readied to leave, his mother kissed her cheeks after his father had hugged her and Gabe laid a smooch or three on her to tease Rafe.

"Belle, I know you'll be with your family on Christmas Day but we'd love to have you for Christmas Eve dinner."

Rafe knew in that moment what it meant. Christmas Eve in the Bettencourt household was sacrosanct. They had dinner, played cards and went to midnight mass. It wasn't something even friends were invited to. It was a family event. Belle, having grown up with them so closely, knew that too and he saw her face as she realized it.

Her hand trembled a bit in his. "I'd be honored to as long as Rafe wouldn't mind."

"I wouldn't want you anywhere else, Annabelle." He kissed her cheek and hugged her.

"All right then. I'll see you day after tomorrow. Thank you for lunch, I'm going to be full for a week."

"Wait until you have Christmas Eve dinner!" Gabe laughed and clapped Rafe on the shoulder, letting him know he supported this next step in the situation with Belle.

He walked her to her car. "Before you say anything let me just tell you I want something with you, Belle. I know you have a job in San Francisco and I'm not asking you to give up your career or your life. I just want to be a part of it. I've known you most of my life and I understand that what I feel for you is real and has been coming a long time. I want you there on Christmas Eve and I want to kiss you as the clock strikes midnight on New Year this year and the next and so on. We on the same page?"

She leaned her forehead against his chest and he struggled to keep quiet as she clearly wrestled with her thoughts. She was not impulsive so he knew the process was hard for her.

"Rafe, I've wanted you for fifteen years. I...I have to deal with my job situation. I can't talk about it just now, I need to get over to my parents' house. But after Christmas, can we just have some time alone to talk? We *are* on the same page in wanting something together. I need to say that up front. I like the idea of you being in my life as more than fantasy material." She looked up at him as she finished, a smile on her lips and he let go of the breath he'd been holding.

"Absolutely. You and me, after Christmas. I'll see you later tonight." He kissed her quickly and she stepped back before they ended up making out in his parents' front drive.

"Man that tree looks great." Belle grinned as she stood back and eyed their handiwork.

"I admit your little diagram helps every year." Kevin laughed. "Although I think one of these years we should just attack it and just put stuff on any old place we want to."

"Tree diagramming is Belle's job. It has been since she was four years old. Your job is staying out of jail and not knocking anyone up until you're twenty-five. We all have our talents." Brian socked Kevin as he handed Belle a mug of spiced cider.

"I'm sure it would look just fine if you put the ornaments on willy-nilly. But it looks even better when everything is distributed evenly and according to a variety of color and also with the new stuff mixing with the older and hand-made ornaments. And don't think I don't know you all have been telling the story about my shoes all around town." Belle snorted and adjusted one of the bows one of them had made in grade school.

"We have this discussion every year. I feel like it's a tradition along with the tree trimming and the garland stringing. Knock it off, Kev and get that stick out of your ass, Belle. The shoe story is fab, it must be told." Chelsea sat and put her feet up with a long sigh.

"You okay?" Belle put her mug down and knelt beside her sister.

"Tired. Doing this at thirty-two is not as easy as it was when I was in my mid-twenties. Home stretch now, I've got three weeks to go and this will be the last trip we take away from home until the baby comes. I'm glad you're here." Chelsea touched her forehead to Belle's.

"I am too. I'm sorry I missed so much this year," she said quietly to Chelsea.

"Promise me you're going to do something about your job." Chelsea's face looked serious.

"It's one of the things I'm thinking about on this vacation. I promise."

"Belle, you gonna tell us all what's going on between you and Rafe?" Brian tossed himself into a chair nearby and at that announcement, the rest of the family gathered near as well.

"Why don't you tell me about Sissy?" Belle countered and Scott burst out laughing.

"What about her? She's a nice girl!" Brian sputtered.

"I didn't say she wasn't so don't get snotty. I haven't been around much, remember? Tell me about her."

"We know about her. What we don't know about is you and Rafe." Kevin waved a hand dismissively at Brian.

"Belle and I are seeing each other. You have a problem with that?" Rafe walked into the room, kissing Belle's mother's cheek and shaking hands with her father before coming straight to Belle's side and dropping to the floor next to her. "Hey, gorgeous." He kissed her quickly, respectfully, on the lips before looking around at everyone else.

"Hi. Did Rosemary get in all right?" Lawd, he made her feel

like a giddy schoolgirl.

"Hello? Am I the only one who didn't know about this?" Belle's father asked.

"*I* had no idea and I'm gonna kick Belle's ass for not telling me!" Chelsea glared at Belle.

"Can we move on please?" Belle asked but Rafe laughed and pulled her so she leaned against him.

"I don't have a problem with it. I think Rafe is a good man. He's very good looking, has a job, a nice house and he's already part of the family." Her mother gave a stern look to the room, daring anyone to disagree.

"Thank you, Mrs. Taylor. Belle and I have known each other a long time, we enjoy each other's company and that's step one. And I'm pretty sure she's going to organize my kitchen very soon."

Belle whacked his arm. Wait 'til he looked in his cabinets at some point. Ha! "Go on and make fun."

"I know you had dinner with your folks but do you have room for some pie, Rafe? I just made a pot of coffee too. Decaf. Would you like some?' Ahh, her mother was the cavalry.

"I think Belle needs some too." Rafe stood, bringing her with him.

"I think Belle is twenty-eight years old and can make her own eating decisions thankyouverymuch." She sent him a censorious look but he just ignored it.

"Come on then, Rafe. You too, Kevin. Let's bring some back for everyone," her mother ordered with a smile on her lips.

They obediently followed their mother and Chelsea grabbed her arm, yanking her back to where she sat. "You so owe me a very long explanation. Have you slept with him and not told me? I thought we agreed that should either of us ever see him naked we'd share?" Chelsea whispered.

Belle burst out laughing and everyone looked in their direction. "I'll tell you tomorrow. Family football game, they'll all be busy and I can give you the details. And they're *good* details, Chels."

"They'd better be so I can forgive you for not telling me sooner."

"It's new! I haven't had the chance to be alone with you for five minutes since it all happened and I wasn't telling you in front of Mom."

"Okay okay, you can tell her all about me when you two are alone. In the mean time, Belle, your mother says to eat every bit of this or she'll spank you." Rafe shoved a huge piece of cherry pie at her.

"This is enough for three people."

"If you'd gone in there with me, you could have cut your own slice." One of his eyebrows arched and she rolled her eyes at him.

The next day at the annual Taylor family football game, Chelsea and Belle sat bundled up, drinking hot chocolate and watching the game while gossiping about Rafe.

"So he just kissed you? Like out of nowhere?" Chelsea asked.

"One minute he's helping me with my bags and the next he and I are standing, face to face in his front hall and he's pressed against me, mouth on my neck and then he laid one on me. Things totally changed right then. Went from friends to something more in a matter of moments. He tells me he wants something more with me, a relationship and I want that too. His family invited me to Christmas Eve and this morning he told me he knows someone who runs a mid-size firm in Sacramento who may be looking for a contracts attorney."

"Really?" Chelsea's eyes widened. "And?"

"He didn't assume he could take over for me. He asked if he could pass on my name. He wants me to be happy in my career. God, Chelsea, that means so much to me. He's not asking that I quit or anything."

"But Belle..."

"I know. I do! It's out of control. My life is out of control and I have to do something. I just need to figure out what. I mean, maybe I can cut back at the firm. There's nothing saying I have to work that hard there. Others don't."

Chelsea didn't say anything but she snorted and later demanded more details about Rafe's talents other than on a football field.

Belle couldn't help but watch him out there playing with her brothers and brother-in-law. It was surreal to see him there and know he was hers in some sense. The night before they'd talked until all hours, laughing and making love.

She'd been halfway in love with him most of her life and every moment they spent together pushed her deeper and deeper with him. At the same time, she'd worked damned hard to achieve all she had and she wasn't about to give it all up for a man. Any man.

"Stop overthinking. I can see the gears turning in your head, Belle," Chelsea chided. "He digs you. You've lusted after him since middle school. Just enjoy it and don't analyze it to death. It's not a freaking thesis project, it's a relationship. You can't diagram love."

Belle huffed out a breath. "I am so sick of people dissing the way I am. Do I make fun of your artistic lifestyle? Do I talk about how financially risky your life is? Have I ever done anything but support you, Chelsea? What right do you have to sneer at the way I organize my thoughts?" She stood up and tossed the blanket on the chair she vacated. "I'm going in."

"Belle! Wait. I'm sorry!"

She heard her sister calling after her but stomped away, not wanting to hear it.

Once she got into the house she heard the phone ringing and grabbed it, eager for something to do before going back outside.

Rafe saw the argument unfold and watched as Belle walked away, torn as to whether he should go after her or not.

"Go on. Just don't push." Brian shoved him in the direction of his gaze and Rafe didn't pause once he'd decided to go.

"Why can't this wait? I'm here with my family for the holidays."

Rafe caught part of her phone conversation.

"This is ridiculous! I haven't had a day off since January, David. This can wait until I get back."

Rafe saw her check her watch and heave a sigh.

"Fine. Fine. No, don't wait for me. Just leave it in my inbox and I'll get it signed today." She hung up and he made noise as he came fully into the room.

She faced him and gave a wan smile. "Hi."

"Can I give you a ride into San Francisco? We could have some alone time and you could show me your place."

She moved to him and took his hands, kissing the fleshy part of his hand below his thumbs. "I need to go. I'll be back later but I have to deal with this paperwork. I shouldn't have answered the phone but...anyway. Thanks for the offer but I need to do this alone."

169

His normally larger than life Belle looked pale and wan. He ached to make things right for her but knew she had to do it herself or she'd never truly come to him. He cupped her cheek. "I'll keep the bed warm for you."

"I won't be that long! I'm just running to the office and coming right back. Three hours at most depending on traffic. Will you tell them? I can't deal right now and I have to go."

"Belle, I won't do your dirty work. I'll tell them but you're going to have to deal when you get back," he said gently.

Her jaw tensed and her smile fell away. "It's not dirty work! This is my job. No one frowns at Brian when he has a patient delivering a baby and leaves during dinner. I won't feel guilty for having achieved something important." She stepped back and he felt a bit colder but he wouldn't let her anger push him. She knew what he meant.

"All right, Belle. I'll see you when you get back. Drive safely." He brushed a kiss over her lips and left her there in the house as he went back out.

Chapter Six

Belle had let anger fuel her all the way until she reached her office door. It was a Saturday, two days before Christmas and during Hanukah and still there were plenty of attorneys working. Mainly the younger ones but doors to the big offices were closed with the lights on so senior partners were there as well.

She stood in her doorway and stared into the space she'd scraped and fought and given up her life for. That small space with the pretty desk and the neatly organized files and utterly clean surface.

The papers David said absolutely had to be signed sat in her inbox. They were, as she thought, something that could have easily waited until her return. She made quick work of them and took them to his secretary's desk, leaving them there and heading to get out as soon as she could. If she took a look at anything else in her inbox she'd end up working and her family deserved her presence and her attention.

"Annabelle, there you are! Say, can you come in for a few minutes and talk with me on this case?" David leaned against his doorjamb.

"No. I thought you were going on vacation." How could she ever have looked up to this man? He *knew* she didn't need to sign those papers, knew she was with her family and he did it just to yank her chain.

"We leave tomorrow. And what do you mean, no?"

"I'm on vacation. My family is expecting me for dinner. I left rather abruptly and I need to get back. I'll speak with you in January when you return." She moved past him toward the elevators and he followed.

"Annabelle, you can't just walk away! This is important."

She hit the down button and waited. "I'm not just walking away. I'm on vacation. I came back to sign those papers and now I'm going back to what I was doing." Belle wanted to smack him but he was, in essence, one of her bosses.

When the elevator came he narrowed his eyes at her, daring her to get on and suddenly, anger that he was just playing power games bloomed within her. She wasn't a freaking thing, she was a person, a damned good attorney.

"Good afternoon, David." She looked unconcerned while the doors closed on his shocked face and then leaned against the wall as she headed to the garage below.

Rafe had left by the time she got back. His whole family had gathered and she knew he would want to be with them. Or so she told herself to not feel so bad he hadn't waited for her.

Instead she tentatively mended fences with Chelsea and ended up staying until nearly midnight, playing cards with Scott and watching old movies. In truth, she allowed herself the feeling of being safe as they lay on the big couch eating popcorn with no light but the jewel tones on the tree.

Scott didn't press her about her job. Didn't harass her about how she looked and didn't try and guilt her over leaving to deal with work. He just hung out with her, hogging the food and let her be. That was his appeal, he was the second oldest of all the siblings and seemed the most comfortable with himself and his place in the world. He worked the farm with Kevin and their father and seemed to love it.

"I need to go home." He finally sat up, stretching.

Belle got up and straightened the room as he put away the movie. After a quick clean up in the kitchen, he walked her to her car and hugged her before they both headed out.

Before she closed her car door, he asked, "Do you want to stay at my apartment tonight? I can sleep on the couch and you can have my bed."

"Thanks, Scott but I'm all right. I just needed some time to think. I'm going straight to sleep."

He laughed. "If you say so but we both know he's going to be waiting for you. He's not a man to just let go of things he wants. And normally, you're not a woman who runs from what's important. So yeah, those are my deep thoughts for the day. I'll see you later."

She laughed as he closed her door.

Just like Scott predicted, Rafe was up watching *It's a Wonderful Life* when she walked in, trying to be quiet.

"Hey," she said quietly, not knowing if Brian was asleep or not.

"Is this where you try to act like there's nothing wrong?" He remained sitting but his eyes didn't miss anything.

"This is where I walked in the door fifteen seconds ago and said hi." She crossed her arms across her chest and looked back at him. "Is this where you try to pick a fight?"

"You're the one who left today and didn't come back until after midnight. Are you saying I shouldn't be angry?"

"What? I was back in less than three hours. *You* were gone when I got back to my parents' house. I've been there all afternoon and evening. You're the one who got all snippy this afternoon. I came back like I said I would. You weren't there and now you have the audacity to accuse me of being at work when all you had to do was *call* my parents' house to see where I was if you were so concerned about it?"

He stalked to where she stood but she didn't give any ground.

"Why didn't you come home?" When he reached for her, she didn't stop him but didn't melt into his embrace either.

"Why didn't you call?"

"We're both being stupid." He kissed the corner of her mouth.

"You're being more stupid than me."

He laughed and led her toward his bedroom.

When Rafe woke up the next morning, Belle wasn't in bed with him. Frowning, he got dressed and went in search of her. He'd traded off with Gabe and their father so he didn't have to be up a four-thirty every morning. Even so, it was just after six and still pretty dark.

The house was quiet and she wasn't in her room or anywhere else he looked. At least her car was still in the driveway.

He felt like shit. He'd overplayed his hand the night before, first by leaving when she hadn't returned in two hours and then by not just at least driving by the Taylors to see if her car was there. A stupid, impulsive and sort of juvenile move on his part.

"So, did you make up with Belle or not?" Brian strolled into the kitchen as Rafe made coffee.

"Mostly. I think. She didn't hit me with a shovel or anything. She's not here though."

"She's probably on a run. She said she wanted to take one but hadn't done it yet. She could use the time in the air and the exercise. What crawled up your ass anyway? I thought you were okay with Belle working." Brian put some bread in the toaster and rooted through the fridge for jam.

Rafe blew out an agitated breath. "I am. But...fuck, she's got this whole other life in San Francisco. A life I'm not a part of. It's rich and urbane and I get up at four-thirty to drive a tractor and oversee fruit picking and cow milking."

"Rafe, do you think she cares about that stuff? She may live in a swank condo in the city but she's a farm girl at heart. And this place isn't exactly a barn you know." Brian indicated the grand kitchen they stood in.

"I don't know. Damn it, I never expected to feel this deeply for her. I mean, I've always loved her like a member of my family and then things began to change five years ago and every time I saw her I resisted but now? I haven't and I'm in love with Belle. Head over heels and I'm a damned cliché."

Brian laughed. "As creeped out as I am by my best friend and my sister sleeping together, you saying that makes me feel a lot better. She needs that grounding influence in her life. She's due to go back to work the day after tomorrow though. What will you do?"

Rafe sighed. "She and I need to talk it through."

"Well, my remodel will be done in a few weeks. It's probably done enough for me to move out now."

"Brian, even if she does accept my proposal, there's room for you until your house is finished."

"Did you just say proposal? You're going to ask her to marry you?" Brian's eyes widened.

"Shit, I did, didn't I?" Rafe shrugged as he realized that was indeed what he said and what he meant. "I know it seems

175

soon."

"Rafe, you've known her since she was a toddler. It's not like you two just met. But you know, she's not impulsive, even when she's known the man proposing to her for over two decades. It'll be interesting." Brian snickered and Rafe tossed a spoon at his head.

The front door opened and closed and Rafe steeled himself. A few moments later Belle came in and he wanted to drop to his knees she was so beautiful.

"Good morning. I take it you went on a run?" He moved to her and kissed her, glad she kissed him back.

"Yeah. I'm rusty. I try to hit the treadmill a few days a week but it's not always possible and man it's cold out there. There was ice on the cars."

Rafe had her sit down and hid his smile when she smoothed out the placemats.

"Let me get you some coffee. I was about to make breakfast, you up for eggs?"

"All those pretty looks and he cooks too. I'm totally in heaven."

"Hey, play your cards right and you can have this every day." Rafe took a risk when he said it but she cocked her head and smiled. Maybe there was hope after all.

They ate breakfast and visited until Brian left to go see some patients and to run errands. Working side by side, Rafe and Belle cleaned the kitchen and that's when he noticed the change in his cabinets.

"Minx. My *organized* little beauty."

"Now you can find your spices. I made a list of the things you needed more of. Some of that stuff is really old. I also took the liberty of tidying up your silverware and cutlery. You know if the knives are all loose in there without being in any order, they'll hit the blades and get dull."

She looked so serious, he kissed the tip of her nose instead of laughing like he wanted to. "Thank you."

"I hope you don't mind me doing that." Her voice had a hesitance and he shook his head.

"I love that you did it for me. I want you to be at home here. And it's not like I'm complaining that you cleaned stuff up."

"I like being here. I like being with you. I'm sorry if I hurt your feelings yesterday by leaving to deal with work shit." She swallowed hard and shook her head. "It wasn't even important. He just yanked my chain because he could."

Anger washed through him at that. "Why would he do that?"

"It's all a power play. Dominance games. It's normal in some firms. It is with mine."

"Belle, I don't want to be judgmental but is that what you want?" He shoved a hand through his hair, annoyed that anyone would toy with her that way.

"I want to take a shower. Can we do that together or do you have someplace to be? We can talk about this afterward. I've been thinking and I have more thinking to do but I really just want to be clean right now and to be with you." The way she asked was so sweet, so vulnerable it nearly broke his heart. For all that strength and ambition, there was a woman in there who faced some big changes and she was scared.

Even if he had to be somewhere he would have tossed it aside to be with her when she asked. He was so in love with Annabelle Taylor his world canted to the side for a moment.

"I don't have to be anywhere but with you. Go ahead on and get the water hot, I'll be in with towels right after you."

She hugged him briefly and he watched as she jogged away, all her best parts jiggling a bit.

She'd stepped into the now hot spray and tipped her head back, letting the water warm her and wash away the morning's run. She wished it could wash away her doubts too.

Every moment she could remember, she'd known what she wanted. She'd made a plan to achieve it. She worked through it and made it a reality and moved to the next thing. Her life was one big to do list and she crossed off achievement after achievement. That's how the universe made sense. Whenever anything felt out of focus, she had her lists and her charts.

But her job was not what it needed to be. God, she actually let that asshole David treat her like shit the day before. For no other reason than that he could.

She hadn't gone to school and worked her ass off to lose contact with her family, work every waking moment and get treated like shit. Especially when she excelled at what she did. She knew she was a damned good attorney and HPG was lucky to have her.

She had a great condo with a spectacular view. The kind of view people dreamed of when they thought of living in San Francisco. But what good was it when she never saw it? Her beautiful furniture and art, the gorgeous sunrises and great neighborhood restaurants were all just a fantasy to her because she was always at work.

Her dream was dissolving and she felt as if she were clinging to smoke. The only real thing in her life was Rafe. When had she fallen in *love* with him? And it was love, she knew that for sure. She supposed it happened day by day and once something romantic unleashed between them, all that love she already felt simply shifted into the spot that'd been waiting for him and only him.

"Mmm, it's Christmas day already. There's a luscious younger woman in my shower. Whatever shall I do with her?" Rafe joined her, his hands immediately caressing her, sliding over her soap-slicked skin until she writhed.

"Have you been good, Rafe?" she asked as she opened her eyes to take in the masculine beauty of his face. The strong, square jaw, the neat, closely trimmed beard and mustache, the full lips and those brown eyes fringed with thick lashes. No man had ever been more handsome in her opinion, than the one currently looking at her like she was the best thing ever.

"I plan to be a lot better in just a minute. Turn around, Belle. Spread your legs and put your hands on the tile when you bend forward."

Shivers ran through her when he repeated back her fantasy from a few nights prior. The cool of the tile in the enclosure was in marked contrast to the humid air and the heat of his hand against her hip as he held her in place.

"I saw you watching me today when I played basketball with the guys, Belle. Did it make you hot?" He thrust into her body in one arch of his hips, filling her instantly and totally.

"Y-yes. Yes, it did." She closed her eyes, her fingers pressing against the tile to find some sort of purchase, emotional and physical, as he surrounded her.

"I thought so. Your nipples were hard when you walked past and you licked your lips. I thought about what they'd feel like wrapped around my cock. Your shorts showed off your legs, cupped your ass and I wanted to follow you into the house and fuck you. We'd have to be quiet because everyone was right outside."

Just like in her fantasy.

He rammed himself into her cunt over and over as she

struggled to breathe. "You're so tight and so wet, I want to feel you without a condom on, Belle. I want to feel the walls of that sweet, hot cunt when my cock is naked."

She wanted that too. Wanted to give him every part of herself.

"You want to touch your clit right now, don't you?"

She nodded vigorously. "Please, you do it," she gasped out.

He fucked into her so hard her breasts bounced and she saw bursts of light behind her closed eyes. He reached around and soapy fingers found her clit. She stuttered a plea for release and his dark chuckle brushed against her ear.

"I love that you're so dirty beneath the silk and cashmere. It's such a turn-on to me, Belle. Your pussy is gorgeous but I don't think I'll last much longer. Come for me, honey, please."

Belle arched her back, taking him deeper and tightened herself around his cock, his fingers on her clit took her higher and higher until spirals of pleasure threaded through her and she came with a soft cry.

"So damned gorgeous," he mumbled as he pressed one last time, deep and she felt the jerk of his cock as he came.

They stumbled from the shower and into bed.

Rafe looked at her skin as the sun fully rose and the house heated. "Do you have to be at work today?" she asked lazily, not opening her eyes.

"I do, but not for a while. Gabe is the guy on point today and tomorrow I have the day off to spend with your family in the morning."

"I'm spending tonight there. They know I'll be in after midnight when I get back from mass with you all. But it's tradition, we all sleep in sleeping bags in the living room. We used to stay up a lot later but now that the boys are old enough, they're up at the crack of dawn and raring to open presents. Would you like to be there too? Share that with me?"

For as long as he'd been essentially part of the Taylor family, he'd never actually spent the night there on Christmas. He'd been with his own family and usually cruised by for brunch after he'd had breakfast with his own crew. But the idea of waking up and making himself part of her tradition after she'd done that with him made him warm inside.

"I'd love that. I don't suppose we'll be able to sneak in each other's sleeping bags and mess around, huh?" He kissed the tip of one breast, breathing her scent in.

She laughed. "Doubtful. All my brothers will be there and while I think they're all okay with us being a couple, I don't think that extends to me giving you a hand-job under the tree."

A surprised laugh bubbled from him. "You can save that one for when we're alone and have our own celebration. Or well, after Brian finally moves into his house again and this place is empty but for you and me." He paused. "Belle, everything is empty without you."

She opened her eyes and turned toward him. "Yeah. But I'm here and if you think I lusted after you for fifteen years so some other chick can lay her hands on you, you're out of your mind. Look, my job situation is really messed up right now. I don't know what to do. But there's one thing I do know and it's that I want to be with you. Of everything right now, it's totally clear to me."

He kissed her for a long time. Just long, lazy meetings of tongue and lips, their breath mingling.

"Good. I want you with me. Do you want to talk about your job?"

To his surprise, she nodded. "Everyone makes fun of me for

being so compulsive and organized but it's what keeps me sane. It's how I manage the world. And so, I have plans for my life. Big ones like becoming a lawyer and even small ones like learning how to do beadwork. I have my list, I check off my goals when I reach them. You know. Anyway, I'm within reach of the top goal on my list for the last eight years. Hell, more than ten years really. In college when I decided I wanted to go to law school I knew what kind of firm I wanted to work at. I knew I wanted to be the best at what I did. When I interned at HPG in law school I knew I wanted the corner office with the view. I knew I wanted *my name* on the letterhead. My own secretary and paralegal, a spot in the garage near the elevators. And so I worked my butt off and it all fell into place goal by goal and I'm within reach now. But I just never imagined the sacrifices. And I'm not talking about hard work, I'm not afraid to work hard."

She said it defiantly, proudly and he saw the farm girl in her right then and it made him warm.

"But I don't have a life. Being here with you and my family only makes that plain. Even though I've been working hard since I graduated, it has only been this last year that it's taken over my entire existence and I'm drowning. I'm losing myself, Rafe. I used to have friends. I used to come home on weekends and even meet Mom halfway for dinner sometimes but I don't do that anymore and everyone has moved on. Chelsea said I'm like a ghost. I don't want to be a ghost! I love my family and I love you."

She sat up, eyes wide and glimmering with unshed tears. He knelt and kissed each eyelid, tasting her. "I love you too."

"Thank God. Anyway, I'm," she sighed, "I guess I'm afraid. And I've not been afraid much in my life really. I'm afraid that for the first time I'm going to have to deviate from a list, make an actual leap. I'm not very brave I guess."

He shook his head and kissed her again. "You're very brave, honey. Change is a scary thing. But you're a damned good lawyer. There are other options out there beside working every waking moment. And I'm behind you, no matter what. If you stay where you are, we'll work it out somehow. Maybe you can negotiate less hours?"

"I don't know. I have to think more about it. But today is Christmas Eve and tomorrow is Christmas and it's all about my favorite people in the world and I'm not going to let this work thing overshadow that. I've never been to midnight mass. Holy cow, I'm nervous to be doing this thing with your family!"

"They all love you, Belle. Why be nervous? You know everyone. Rosemary was in your year in school. Gabe thinks you hang the moon and my mother just giggles to herself that I'm bringing home a woman she thinks is worthy."

Her eyes narrowed. "Oh? Have you brought home unworthy women for Christmas before, Raphael? Like, say Sarah Munson?"

How the hell did she know about that? He shifted, torn between discomfort and wanting to laugh at how sweet she was when she was jealous. "Sarah and I have been broken up for eight months. And I'll have you know I never brought her home for anything much less something important like Christmas Eve. Belle, honey, none of us has ever brought home a sweetheart for Christmas Eve. Even if I'd wanted to invite her, which I didn't, my mom is the one who invites. That should be a big signal to you. Hell, she didn't invite Ben until after he and Rosemary were engaged. You're the first girlfriend to ever actually be invited. So see, you're in, honey."

"Yeah, nothing like knowing that to make me feel better! Oh my God! I need a new dress. The stores will be insane but I'll just go now and deal with it." She rushed to get out of bed but he pulled her back.

"You will not. Don't be silly. You're beautiful and you'll be just fine in what you have. Now, I'll meet you here at six, all right?"

They arranged to meet later and both went their separate ways for the day.

Chapter Seven

Instead of heading over to her parents', she went back to her condo for a while. She needed to grab a more appropriate dress for that night with the Bettencourts and she needed to think.

When she turned on her laptop, over forty messages from David about meaningless stuff popped up. He'd also given her home and cell number to one of their clients who'd called to bother her about an issue he knew very well she couldn't get an answer on until after the new year. Two other partners she did work for on a regular basis had also called and her stress level began to spike.

She stood in her living room, holding her cell phone in her hands and shaking with the desire to call and answer emails even though it was a short damned vacation and the answers were meaningless at that point.

Heaving a sigh, she walked through her place. It was beautiful and she could only barely afford it but she'd splurged and bought the small condo overlooking the water in the distance. Gleaming tile and chrome made her feel serene. Or it had at one point but all she could think about was the warm Spanish tile in Rafe's kitchen and the open, airy feel of the very large house. By contrast, the condo stifled and it felt like she couldn't sit or breathe for fear of making a mess.

When it'd happened that her white carpet and spotless tile became less comforting than the jumble of colors and noise of Rafe's house she couldn't say. The suddenness of it startled her and she sat rather abruptly in the middle of her kitchen.

She'd thought the Kitchen Aid mixer was the epitome of success when she'd bought it. A status marker that she was a grown up professional woman. Her dinnerware had been imported from Italy and the china from England. It wasn't the cost so much, but the way she'd been able to take a step up each time she'd hit a new high in her career.

But it all fell from her grasp as she realized none of it mattered. Yes, being a damned good attorney mattered. Being successful mattered to her very much. But what she had wasn't success, it was slowly siphoning her life, her personality away.

Shame washed through her as she realized she'd let her job eat up her life and take over her identity. That wasn't what she wanted at all. She didn't want to exchange a corner office for her family and she sure as hell didn't want to give up time spent with Rafe, in his arms and at his side in their community, for her name on letterhead.

She stood with new resolve and felt better than she had in three years.

When she walked into her parents' house sometime after noon her mother merely smiled serenely at her. "Well now, did you have a late night?"

"I was here until midnight watching movies with Scott. And I went on a run and had some quality time with Rafe this morning before he had to get to work and I ran to my place to grab a few dresses for tonight. I need your opinion."

She held one outfit, a deep red wrap dress that came to her mid-calf, to her body. "I'd wear this one with those boots I got a few years back. You know the black ones with the nice heel?"

"Hmm, that's a good color for you too. Makes your skin look pretty, highlights your hair. I do love those boots too and you'll be nice and warm." Her mother looked her up and down. "What else do you have?"

"Black is always good, right?" She pulled out a black cashmere dress with buttons up the front, this one a bit shorter than the red one. "I have a few scarves I can accessorize with and a few different heels to choose from depending on which scarf I choose."

"Go with the first one. It's prettier I think." Chelsea came in and sat on a stool at the counter.

The air between them was still a bit unsettled since their spat the afternoon before. They'd only begun to tentatively mend things last night but Belle knew they'd be all right.

"Is it okay to wear red to mass?"

Her mother laughed. "It's not a really conservative church and it is Christmas Eve so the red would work just fine. It's not slutty red, it's not overly revealing. It's classic and feminine and totally what I'd love to see a daughter-in-law-to-be wearing to an audition dinner."

"Holy cow, Mom! Don't say stuff like that. I'm nervous enough as it is. Rafe told me he loved me today and that none of them has ever had a sweetie home for Christmas Eve before." Belle hung the dresses up in the hall closet and returned to the kitchen where her mother had poured her some cranberry juice.

"We're making gingerbread houses with the kids, come on then. Look, Annabelle, of course he loves you. I can't believe I never noticed the way he looked at you before. And of course Beatriz and Anthony love you, you're already a member of their family. Don't be anyone other than yourself. It's not a job interview. You'd wear that black dress to a business dinner.

You wear the red to a family holiday dinner. You're Belle, the very organized woman their son is lucky to have landed." Chelsea hugged her, their fight forgotten.

"Now come on, I only came in here to get more gumdrops and the kids will riot if we're gone too long. Maybe you can help. They're fighting and everyone wants to do the same part of the job." Her mother grabbed Belle's arm and pulled her into the dining room where her nephews and the younger children of her cousins had a huge assembly line set up.

"This smells good! Why don't we all just eat the gingerbread and forget about the houses?" Chelsea came in and the kids gasped.

Belle stepped in and began to set up little stations, assigning the kids a specific job on the assembly line so they'd stop arguing over who did what. Within a few moments the bickering had stopped and things were moving along.

"Hmm, sometimes being anal retentive isn't a bad thing, now is it?" Belle winked at Chelsea.

"Totally."

After the houses were made and the gingerbread people were decorated and eaten, Belle took the kids out back with her brothers and they ran them like puppies until they were so exhausted they didn't have the energy to fight.

Instead, they huddled on the big couches in the living room with snacks and blankets and watched the same version of Rudolph she and her siblings had watched. Burl Ives' narration and wooden puppets always made her nostalgic.

"I gotta say how cool it is to see the next generation out there. This is my favorite time of year. All the people I love are right here with me. Belle, sweetie, I've missed you so much this year." Her mother hugged her. "I am so proud of you for making this dream of yours a reality, I am. But I am sad that you're going back home day after tomorrow and we may not see you for another year or more. It breaks my heart."

"Mom, trust me on this, okay? I've done a lot of thinking and it breaks my heart too. Just give me some time and trust me. Now, I need to get back to Rafe's to get changed for dinner."

She grabbed the presents for the Bettencourts, promised to see everyone when they got back from mass and headed out with her dress.

Rafe looked Belle up and down and seriously regretted having to share her with anyone. The shade of red she had on was gorgeous and she looked amazing with her hair hanging in loose waves, held back from her face with some sort of fancy band thing on her head.

"Those boots are quite the thing, honey. You'll need to wear them for me again when I can have you to myself all night long."

She blushed, making him laugh.

"What?"

"I love that you blush when, honey, you have the dirtiest mind of any woman I've ever met. It's seriously sexy."

She wound her arms around his neck and kissed him. "Oh, why thank you. I'm glad it doesn't freak you out. I've never really, you know, let it all go before with anyone so I'm relieved you didn't think I was a skank."

His hands slid down the curve of her back and cupped her ass. "Belle, you couldn't be a skank even if you dressed as one for Halloween. You're a lady through and through. Tough, smart, good hearted, organized and when the door closes and you let your hair down, you're hot and not a little naughty. Truly, the perfect combination. Now, let's go before I fuck you right here in the hall and my mother comes looking for us."

They drove over and he held her hand the entire time. Funny how she'd simply fit into a spot in his life he hadn't really known was empty but there she was, sitting in the passenger seat, his truck filled with her presence, filled with *them* in a way he knew was right.

"Crap! Rafe, how many people are here?" She sat up straight as they pulled up the long drive to the house. Cars filled every available space.

"There are probably seventy-five people here tonight. My dad always has to bring out all the table leaves and my aunt and uncle and other relatives bring extra tables and chairs. A house full of people who all know about you. Just saying that up front. You know a lot of them and they love you already. The ones you don't will once they meet you. And my grandma is here."

"You never told me that, Rafe." Belle fanned her face and looked panicked. "Rafe, the only exposure I've had to her has been glimpses when she visits every other year. I've never met her! I have to admit, I'm scared of her."

"My grandmother is very nice, don't look scared. She'll love you. She's just a bit, um, well yeah. Anyway, you'll love her and she'll love you but she's going to pretend she only speaks Portuguese until she gets to know you." He got out quickly and ran around to her side to open her door before she could reply.

"I'll get even for this," she said in an undertone.

He grabbed the gigantic bag filled with presents he told her not to buy to begin with and shook his head at her defiant look. Giving in and grinning, he took her hand in his free one and they headed in.

The house was insane with activity. Four generations of Bettencourts and Pereiras swarmed the place. He caught sight of his grandmother holding court in the living room, surrounded by grandchildren and great-grandchildren. She caught sight of him and smiled, waving him over.

Keeping a tight grip on Belle's hand he dropped the bag of presents near the tree, knowing she was probably having a stroke that he didn't take them from the bag and lay them out nicely. He tugged her toward his grandmother, thankful his mother saw them and moved in their direction to head off any potential trouble.

He knelt and kissed his grandmother's cheeks, speaking to her in rapid-fire Portuguese, telling her who Belle was and how special a person she was to him. His mother nodded, adding her own observations.

Belle stood and smiled at the scene, she'd met many of the people there at least a few times, as Brian and Rafe were so close. Really, it was pretty much like her house at a holiday. Kids running around, a cat hiding under the couch, rich scents of yummy stuff coming from the kitchen and people just happy to be with each other, or pretending to in some cases.

She also tried to pretend she didn't know they were all talking about her. Belle made a mental note to get herself some Portuguese language tapes. She knew bits and pieces, enough to say please and thank you, she knew how to ask for bread and that sort of thing. But beyond that, she was lost.

"Hey there, Annabelle!" Rafe's little sister, Rosemary, came and hugged her.

"Rosemary, man you look marvelous! I love the new hairdo."

Rosemary touched her hair with a smile. "Thanks. Ben was worried about it being short but with two kids and a third on the way, the long hair just wasn't worth the hassle for me. I hear you're seeing Rafe? It's about time!"

Belle laughed, keeping her ear tuned to the conversation

with Rafe's grandmother so when it was time, she could meet her and not appear rude.

"Don't worry, she's really a cool old woman. She just likes to play the boys off like this. Be yourself, she'll like you," Rosemary whispered of her grandmother.

"Belle." Rafe stood and touched her arm and she turned to face his grandmother with a smile. A smile the older woman returned, a bit of mischief in her eyes.

"This is my grandmother, Lourdes Pereira. Grandma, this is Annabelle Taylor."

Belle knelt so she faced Lourdes and held out her hand. "It's an honor to meet you, Mrs. Pereira. Raphael and his brothers and sister speak of you often."

Lourdes nodded and looked to Rafe, who hadn't bothered translating. She snorted and looked back to Belle. "I was going to be threatening and old, like my husband's grandmother did to me but I decided I like the look of you. Beatriz tells me you're a good girl and Raphael tells me he loves you and has known you most of your lives. I like that. I don't come around often. But next time we see each other, you'll speak Portuguese to me."

Belle stifled the urge to gulp and kick the carpet. Instead she laughed and nodded. "Yes, ma'am. And I love Raphael too. I have since I was a teenager. Only he never looked at me twice."

At that, Belle found herself seated next to Lourdes the entire evening. For dinner and dessert afterward, she told Belle all manner of great stories about growing up in the Azores and then coming to the United States to meet the man she was to marry, Rafe's grandfather who later died in the Korean War.

When they moved to the living room after the mess from dinner was cleaned up, Belle sat, snuggled up to Rafe. This was more important than letterhead any old day. He'd reminded her without preaching it. He'd simply let her see it.

It took some time to get through the presents, even with several people taking the used paper out of the way and Rafe's father and uncle handing out the presents in shifts.

Belle received several presents much to her surprise and delight, including a hand-knitted wrap she planned to wear that very night when they left for mass.

"One last one, Belle," Rafe said. "Well not last, there are more from me at your parents' house for the morning." He laughed. "But for now, well." He stood and brought her with him. "Five years ago I saw you at your law school graduation and suddenly you weren't that annoying little control freak sister of my best friend. Something had changed and that day is when I started falling in love with you. I told myself it was silly, Brian would kick my butt if he knew and then we both worked so much I didn't see you as often as I'd wished to even start something with you. But a few days ago and some mistletoe let me finally realize what I'd known all along. I love you, Belle Taylor and I want us to be together. I want you to be my wife and share my life. Be here with me for the good times and the bad and bear our children. I want that with you, I want there to be an us tomorrow and for all the rest of our days."

Belle blinked back tears. She couldn't believe what she was hearing.

"I know! I know it seems sudden but you know me and I know you. I've known you since I was eight years old and you were four. I've been a part of every major important day in your life and the same goes for you. You know what I believe in and you hold those beliefs as well. I respect your drive and ambition. I love that you iron towels and organize my spices. Make my house a home, Belle. Say yes."

It wasn't sudden. Not really. He was right, he'd been her

friend for decades, a member of her family and certainly a man who'd held her erotic and romantic imagination for years. Rafe Bettencourt was her fantasy man come true. He was real.

"I'm so not an impulsive person. You know that. I do most things on a schedule and I keep endless lists and yes, I iron tea towels and organize spices. Marriage is on my list you know. The big life list I have laminated and in my wallet. It's on the schedule for three years from now."

Rafe stared at her and she grinned.

"But I guess I'll have to laminate a new one because marriage just moved up the list and I'll have to cross it off."

"Is that a yes?"

She nodded. "If you'll have a very organized contracts lawyer as your wife."

He huffed out a sigh of relief as the room let out a whoop of celebration. "Belle, you had me going there for a bit with all that talking."

"Yeah, I know. But I can't have everyone always thinking I'm predictable now can I?"

He dropped to one knee and opened a velvet pouch into his palm. Two rings slid out, glittering in the lights from the tree and the lit candles in the room.

"These were my great-grandmother's rings. My grandmother brought them with her so I could give them to you. Then our grandson can give them to his wife-to-be. Will you wear them?"

She held out a trembling hand as he slipped on a very beautiful opal and diamond ring. "It's gorgeous." Feminine and classic. The ring fit her style perfectly.

"The band we'll save for the wedding."

"Gosh, the watch I got for you just doesn't quite measure up," she said quietly as they pulled up in her parents' driveway after mass.

"Belle, you agreed to marry me. That's way better than anything I've ever gotten."

"We should have stopped by your house like I said. I hate that I won't be naked with you until tomorrow night."

He helped her out of the car, grabbing her overnight bag. Bending down, he captured her lips for a kiss. "Tomorrow once we get to *our* house, I'm going to have you every way I can think of. For now, let's just pray your mother doesn't kill me for asking you to marry me without her there."

"Yeah, that's going to be a close call. But I think you'll be all right. She likes you." Belle laughed quietly but she needn't have bothered as everyone seemed to still be up when they went into the house.

More insanity when Belle's mother, who'd been making hot chocolate for everyone, caught sight of Belle's ring after she'd changed into her pajamas and came out into the living room.

"Is that what I think it is, Annabelle?"

"If you think it's an engagement ring, yep. Rafe asked me to marry him and I said yes." Belle grinned as people got up and rushed at her and Rafe, hugging and kissing cheeks, slapping shoulders and congratulating them.

"You move fast! Why didn't you tell me you planned to do this tonight?" Belle's mother demanded of Rafe.

"I just decided yesterday to ask her so soon. My grandmother brought the rings because I knew I wanted to ask Belle to marry me but I'd planned to wait until Valentine's Day." He shrugged and hugged Belle. "But yesterday it just hit me that it was time. I'd wasted five years knowing she was everything I ever wanted in a woman so I decided to stop wasting time and marry her."

They stayed up until nearly two-thirty, talking, planning and laughing. Finally everyone snuggled down in sleeping bags and decided to try and sleep before the kids woke up at the crack of dawn.

Chapter Eight

It'd been a good day with the Taylors. Rafe knew they'd accepted him, not just in the way they had before but as their daughter's soon-to-be husband.

He'd watched while she played with the wooden block set her youngest nephew had received, while she rubbed Chelsea's back and had run around, taking care of people.

They'd had a huge lunch and half his family had come over to join them and much talk about consolidating Easter had begun.

Finally, it was nearly nine that night when they escaped. He hesitated to even bring up what would happen the next day. He was mulling over how to broach the subject when she bypassed his house and got on the freeway instead.

"We're going to my condo for a bit. We'll talk when we get there, all right?"

He wondered if she planned to sleep there so she could get to work early the next morning and told himself that was all right. He'd work around her schedule. It wouldn't be easy, but he'd commute back to Davis if he had to.

Instead, he'd simply stared, utterly dumbfounded when they'd walked in her front door.

"This is your house? Wow, Belle, this is like a spread in one of those home magazines. God, I hope I don't stain your carpets."

"You won't be here long enough for that to be a worry."

"Belle, if you think you're going to live here while I live in Davis and I see you once a year, you've got another thing coming. I'll live here and commute every day. I can work it with Gabe so I won't always have to be out there so early. And the reverse commute isn't going to be that bad." He put his hands on his hips and dared her to argue.

Instead she burst into tears and threw herself into his arms.

"What? What is it, honey? Don't cry. We'll work it out. I'm okay with you working, I promise." He rubbed a hand up and down her back.

"No, not that. Rafe, you'd give up hours of your day, every day to live here, in a tiny condo with white carpets when you have a huge house a mile from your job? I love you so much. I can't believe you're mine." She smiled up at him and he smiled back.

"Of course I would. Belle, I love you. I'd rather be with you and commute than not be with you. Even for ten minutes a day."

"Well that's not necessary. I stopped over here yesterday to get the dress I wore last night and I thought a good long time about my life. And my job sucks. I hate to admit it, it was on my list and it's a hugely important firm and all that. But I handed in my letter of resignation yesterday. I have some stuff to tie up and it'll take me a month or so, but I'll work on my resume and look for something in Sacramento or even Davis. I don't want to trade my life for a job. Especially now that you're in it." Belle took a breath and watched his face as he realized what she'd said.

"That's...are you sure, Belle? I don't want you to have regrets over me. Not ever."

"I'd already started to think about another job before last week. Being with you, being reminded about what's truly important is what helped me make my choice. I have no regrets. I do however, have until January second for vacation. I took those days as well and I'll be able to cash out a lot more. So you'll kiss me at midnight and I'll wake up in your arms in the new year and every day after that too."

He picked her up and swung her in a circle, laughing. "Let's grab some of your stuff to move into our place. Thank God Brian will be out soon so we can have it all to ourselves."

When she fell asleep that night, nestled into his side, she was tired, but not the kind of tired she'd come home with. A good kind of tired from a day filled with joy and laughter.

The sound of an alarm brought Belle out of her deep sleep.

"Shh. Go back to sleep, Belle. It's early."

She started, adrenaline shooting through her system, waking her up. When she rolled over she was face to face with none other than a very naked, very sexy Rafe Bettencourt. Her fiancé. How cool was that?

"Morning, gorgeous. It's only four-thirty. Go back to sleep." He leaned in to kiss her lips softly but she grabbed his shoulders, holding him to her.

With a groan, he pulled her against his body, making her well aware he was very happy to see her.

"Well that's a very fine good morning. You going to get up and check on cows with me?"

Belle saw the flash of his grin in the low light.

"No, you're going to fuck me so I have a nice memory in my dreams until I wake up at a decent hour." She stretched into his body and he traced a fingertip over her lip and down the line of her neck.

"Well what's stopping you?" She sat up. "Wait, I'll be right back!" Belle hustled into the bathroom, took care of business and brushed her teeth before getting back to him.

"Crap it's cold." She shivered, her teeth chattering.

"I know, I just turned the heat up. Come here and let me warm you." A large, warm hand grabbed her hip and pulled her toward its owner. Rafe kissed down her neck and across her collarbone, his hands gently kneading her shoulders, turning her into a puddle of goo.

"You're good at that," she sighed, running her hands up his arms, over his biceps. "And my God do you have an amazing body."

He laughed softly, just before tracing her left nipple with the tip of his tongue. Pleasure, slow and warm, oozed through her system as he sucked the nipple into his mouth, his teeth grazing it lightly.

Her hips rolled without conscious thought on her part, seeking contact with him.

"Patience, Belle. You're so soft and sweet. We have a lifetime of morning sex before the sun rises." He kissed the sensitive skin between her breasts, the dark silk of his hair tickling her nipples.

"Fuck patience, Rafe." She shoved his shoulders and rolled atop him with a laugh of triumph as her hair surrounded them both.

"Any more fantasies you want to share?" He waggled his brows in the low light.

"Do you really want to talk right now?" She looked down at him, chest heaving. Her pussy hovered over his cock, sliding along the shaft. Little bursts of pleasure skittered through her as the crown nudged over her clit.

"We'll talk later. Give me what you've got, Annabelle Louise."

Rafe gave over to her ministrations without a fight. If Belle wanted to be on top he certainly had no problem letting that happen. She liked to be in control and also liked it when he was. He could definitely be just fine with that kind of easygoing attitude from his sweet control freak.

Her hair slid over his face and neck as her lips and tongue drew over the tendons in his neck. She scooted down, the molten heat of her pussy teasing over his cock until he thought he'd die.

He gasped when the edge of her teeth scraped over his nipples, first one and then the other. She teased the other with her fingers while her mouth kept him hypnotized. Admittedly, he'd never thought of his own nipples as much of an erogenous zone but after several interludes with Belle, he'd totally rethought that.

He marveled at the curve of her spine as he stroked over each nub of her vertebrae with his fingertips. So soft and yet he knew she was sturdy and strong.

The heat of her mouth slid down his chest and over his stomach. He couldn't help but hiss in surprise and pleasure when she nipped at his belly button. She drew her hair across his lower stomach and then across his cock.

He still couldn't quite get over how wild she was in bed. Just thinking about it during the days made him hard, made him want to drop everything and find her, see what they could get up to.

Reaching back, he stacked the pillows behind his head so he could watch as she lowered her mouth over his cock. He centered all his attention on how she took him into her mouth. When she looked up and locked eyes with him as she continued to suck his cock, a gasp burst from his lips at how exposed he felt. The moment was intensely intimate.

"Belle, honey, that feels so good." He let himself be lured by her eyes, by the way her mouth looked as she swallowed him, by the way her pale skin contrasted with his as she held the base of his cock.

He sifted his fingers through her hair, loving the way it felt, cool and soft. The room was warming up from the heat and what the two of them generated together.

Too close. He didn't want to come anywhere but deep inside her. He touched her shoulder. "Belle, wait. I don't want to come right now. Come up here."

With a frown she lifted and let go, leaving a parting kiss before crawling up his body. "I wasn't done."

"No you aren't, honey. I promise you that." He leaned over and turned on the bedside lamp and perused the line of her body in the brighter light the lamp provided. "So damned pretty. On your back, it's my turn to return the favor."

"You'd better finish the job though."

He laughed. "Naked and sassy, my favorite kind of woman."

Before she could reply, he slid down the bed and between her thighs, pushing her open and baring her pussy to his gaze. His mouth watered to see her like that, glistening and ready for him.

Petting over her closely trimmed curls, he lowered his face to her and she arched with a gasp. Her taste seduced him, spice and salt, sweet and tang. Uniquely her and totally delicious. He'd savor her for hours when he got home from work later but he had to have her right then or he'd die. He needed to make her come and slide deep. The memory would sustain him until he could sneak away later to be with her again.

As he licked over the furls of her pussy, he slid two fingers into her and hooked them, stroking her sweet spot as he drove her higher and higher.

"Yes," she cried out. He heard her moans and the way her fingers dug into his shoulders, he knew she was getting closer.

She writhed beneath him, whimpering and begging. The muscles in her thighs trembled against his biceps. One hand fucking into her, the other holding her open to him, he set to business, pressing the flat of his tongue over her clit and sliding it from side to side.

"Sweet baby Jesus on a skateboard," she whispered as her body spasmed around his fingers and she came.

Her eyes widened as he slid the fingers he'd had inside her into his mouth and hummed his appreciation. "I can't get enough of you, Belle. I know that I could take you three times a day until I die and it still wouldn't be enough."

"You're really good at this stuff," she said, breathless.

He rolled over and fished around next to the pillow and found the condom she'd brought back from the bathroom. "Always prepared. I love that about you."

Belle took it from him and ripped it open, rolling the latex on his cock quickly. "I don't think they had merit badges for this one. Soon, this won't be necessary. I can't wait."

"Me either, honey. For now, ride me," he urged, voice hoarse with desire.

She nodded and her eyes darkened as she straddled him and slid down the length of his cock.

Every nerve ending in his body sang out as her velvety heat

surrounded him in a tight embrace. He looked up at her, at the gentle sway of her breasts as she moved up and down. She was a sight, half-closed eyes, full lips swollen from his kisses. Unbelievably beautiful.

Belle moved so she'd be able to run her hands over the hard belly. Christ on a cracker, the man had the hardest stomach and it was furry in all the right places. No waxing but he was nicely manscaped around his cock. The right mix of masculinity and thinking about who'd be down there. Well, hmpf, no one but her from now on.

"Belle? Are you okay? You look funny. Am I hurting you?"

She looked down at him and laughed. "I'm fine. Just thinking about your body and how good you look naked. And how much I love you and can't believe *the* Rafe Bettencourt is my boyfriend." She laughed and he joined in.

"Well, I'm glad I please you. You're a damned gorgeous sight yourself. And not your boyfriend, your man. Your husband if you'd just pick a damned date."

"These things take time! They have to be planned. I have a lot of work to do. Don't distract me, we're fucking. I'll think about the wedding later and if you suggest Vegas again, I'll punch you."

He put his hands up in defense. "No ma'am. I'm all yours."

Needing him deeper, she brought her hands to her calves, arching her back and changing her angle. She knew it was good for him too by the way he groaned and reached up to caress her thighs, moved to take the weight of her breasts, such as they were, into his hands. His thumbs flicked back and forth over her nipples, making her pussy clench each time he did it.

He felt so good, deep inside her, stretching her and filling her all at once. His hands on her did all the right things. Or maybe it was just the fact that the moment was wish fulfillment of nuclear proportion. Whatever it was, it was hot and spectacular and nothing else she'd ever received for Christmas could match Rafe and his proposal.

He kept one hand on her breast while the other trailed down her stomach to the point where they were joined. Drawing the slickness from her pussy up, he slid a finger 'round and 'round her clit.

She'd thought she'd be incapable of coming again so quickly but apparently not.

"Come again for me, Belle. Don't send me out into the cold without the pleasure of watching you have another orgasm. You're so sexy when you fly apart."

He said it right as he touched her clit with the tip of his finger, just a feather of a touch but enough. He arched up into her pussy deep and hard.

A ragged cry tore from her lips as she came, muscles pulsing and grasping at him. It pulled him down with her, the muscles in his neck corded, hips thrusting as he met her downstrokes onto him.

She forgot everything but the way she felt with him there for long minutes.

"Holy crap," he gasped as she collapsed down beside him.

"Yeah," she croaked, her voice hoarse, mouth dry.

He got up and dealt with the condom, returning to her quickly. "I have to get moving, honey. I'm sorry. I wish I could stay here with you for the next few hours but we're trying out some new equipment today."

"I understand. I'm spending the day with my mom and sister. You need someone to scrub your back?" She winked and he laughed, pulling her to the bathroom with him.

About the Author

To learn more about Lauren Dane, please visit www.laurendane.com. Send an email to Lauren at laurendane@laurendane.com or stop by her message board to join in the fun with other readers as well. www.laurendane.com/messageboard

Look for these titles by *Lauren Dane*

Now Available:

Chase Brothers Series:
Giving Chase
Taking Chase
Chased
Making Chase

Cascadia Wolf Series:
Wolf Unbound
Standoff
Fated

Reading Between The Lines

Coming Soon:

Sweet Charity
Always

GREAT
cheap
fun

Discover eBooks!

THE FASTEST WAY TO GET THE HOTTEST NAMES

Get your favorite authors on your favorite reader, long before they're
out in print! Ebooks from Samhain go wherever you go, and work with
whatever you carry—Palm, PDF, Mobi, and more.

Samhain
Publishing
Ltd

WWW.SAMHAINPUBLISHING.COM

Printed in the United States
129931LV00003B/64/P